Highland Avenue

Highland Avenue

A NOVELLA

To Vicky
Happy Birthday
Enjoy *Natalie*

Natalie Grude Harrington

Kudzu Editions
Alpharetta, Georgia

Kudzu Edtions
P.O. Box 5005
Alpharetta GA 30023

ISBN: 978-0-9963492-0-8
Library of Congress Control Number: 2015939770

Cover Photo by permission of Archives and Collections, Georgia State Library, Atlanta, Georgia

Colorization: Tom Dell
Cover Design: Laura Ellis
Author Photo: M. M. Self

10 9 8 7 6 5 4 3 2   0 4 2 8 1 5

Printed by BookLogix
Alpharetta, Georgia

∞ This paper meets the requirements of ANSI/NISO Z39.48-1992 (Permanence of Paper)

*This book is dedicated to
two people who were always there for me:
my father Sam Grude and my brother Gary Grude.*

*They cared for me, protected me,
and gave me unconditional love.*

*I miss them both every day that I live, and I live
in hope that we may someday be together again.*

Many people will walk in and out of your life, but only true friends will leave footprints in your heart.

—Eleanor Roosevelt

Chapter One

When Sam Robkin awoke, he was confused, not quite knowing where he was. This had been happening a lot lately. It was well past dawn outside, but because of the closed blinds of his bedroom window the room was almost totally dark. He reached across to the other side of the bed, just as he had done every morning for more than sixty years. He then quickly realized once more that he was alone in the bed. The warm comfortable feel of Hannah, his wife for more than sixty years, was no longer there. She had died almost three years before but he still continued to reach for her. He supposed he always would.

Sam stretched and yawned and tried to come fully awake. The house was still and quiet as it always was, and why not? He was the only one in it to make any kind of noise.

Now, as he was coming awake, he was surprised to notice that he wasn't feeling his usual aches and pains:

the arthritis in his joints, the needling feeling in his feet, and all the other little points of discomfort were somehow not there.

Earlier in the week his daughter had taken him to her orthopedist. The doctor gave him cortisone shots and a prescription for another pain medication. The doctor emphasized that any relief he felt would be only temporary.

Temporary or not, Sam was pleased with how well he felt. "Today, maybe," he said to himself, "will turn out to be a good day."

He tried to remember what day of the week it was. They all seemed to be the same now. His son-in-law had pointed out to him that when you turn the cable on it gives you the date and time.

Sam reached over to the small bedside table where he kept his eyeglasses. He put his glasses on. His hand went to the same table and found the television remote without fumbling for it. Sam prided himself on being a man leading an orderly life. Every night before going to sleep he put down his eyeglasses and the remote in the same exact places.

He clicked on the small black-and-white Zenith that was on top of the bureau across the room. The light from the TV screen made the room suddenly brighter. The night before he had finished his day with David Letterman as he had been doing for years (and for years before Letterman with Johnny Carson). Because he would leave the TV tuned to the same channel before turning it off at night, he knew the *Today* show would be on as soon as he clicked on the TV in the morning.

The date and time appeared. It was just a little before eight. He heard Katie Couric happen to mention that it was Wednesday. "Wednesday," Sam said aloud. That reminded him that DelRee would be coming that day. DelRee had been working for his family for more than forty years. She had helped raise his children along with Hannah and himself. She had always been more than an employee, never being considered just a maid. She was part of the Robkin family. Sam hoped she felt the same way, too.

His daughter had insisted that he have DelRee come three days a week. This was really because she wanted someone with him at least some of the time since he was determined to stay in his house. Sam and his daughter had a running argument about her wanting him to sell the house and move in with her.

"So far," Sam thought, "I'm winning the argument." Having DelRee come three days a week was a concession he had finally made. His daughter originally had wanted DelRee to come every day.

The arrangement would do for now. Besides, her coming in a few days a week gave DelRee some extra income, since all she had was her Social Security check each month. The little envelope of cash his daughter gave her every two weeks had to help.

DelRee's actual duties were light—a little dusting, every so often running the vacuum cleaner, and now and then some washing and ironing. There was no one else in the house to make a mess. Most of the time he used only some of the rooms: the den with his lounge chair and the big television, his bathroom, his bedroom, and the kitchen. Whenever he finished using the kitchen he cleaned up after himself just as he had always done.

DelRee nowadays did very little in the way of cooking for Sam. In the past she had prepared almost all of the family's meals, especially when the kids were young. Her specialty was fried chicken and homemade biscuits. She would bake a lot of sweet things in those days, too. When the kids came home from school, DelRee always had treats for them—cookies, a piece of cake, or a slice of pie, always with tall glasses of cold milk.

DelRee's hours at Sam's house now were a restful time, a reward in a way for all the labor she had put in when the house was so much busier, back when the kids were growing up. DelRee now spent a lot of time watching TV with Sam. She remarked often how much she loved watching Oprah every afternoon.

Sam smiled recalling this. He loved watching Oprah's show, too.

Thinking about DelRee, especially memories of her cooking, made Sam realize how hungry he felt. He always felt hungry in the morning. As a rule, after his dinner in the evening Sam never ate another bite until breakfast.

He had always fretted a bit about his weight and had always eaten sensibly. As a young man he had been diagnosed with an ulcer and that, too, had made him very conscious of what food and how much of it he ate. The fact that he couldn't exercise the way he once did also made him think carefully about calories. There had been a time years back when he was slightly overweight, on his way to being what he thought of as pudgy. It was then that he took up walking as a way to keep his weight in balance. His main exercise over the years had been long, brisk walks. Up until his late seventies he had put in many miles a day.

He really missed those walks. "Maybe today," he thought, "I'll feel free from pain. Maybe today I can take a walk again, maybe a lot slower than before and maybe not so long, but still a good walk."

Not being able to take his long walks had made Sam even more conscious of how he managed his diet and the importance of eating sensibly. There was a time in his younger days when the kids were little he used to eat lots of eggs, red meat, sweets, and especially good bread. He had often remarked that the bakeries in Atlanta never had bread like the bakeries in New York, not to mention bagels, much less cheesecake.

Nowadays his daughter cooked much of the food he ate. She shopped for him, and on Saturdays she brought over what she had prepared for him. She loaded up his refrigerator with dishes he could microwave—favorites like noodle kugel, baked apples, and chicken noodle soup. Each week she would take home the Tupperware containers from the week before that DelRee had washed for her.

Sam sat on the side of the bed getting his bearings, and was pleased to note that he didn't make his usual little groan as he leaned over to put on his slippers. Still in his pajamas, he pulled on his old blue bathrobe and took his cane that he always kept hooked over the headboard of his bed. "At least," he thought, "I don't have to use one of those walkers with split yellow tennis balls on the front legs yet."

He walked slowly to the bathroom to wash up and shave. He had never liked shaving but always did his best, just as he had all his years as a salesman, presenting to the world a clean-shaven face except for his always neatly clipped mustache. Sam never wanted to be one of those old men walking around with stubble on their cheeks and chin. His skin had always been sensitive, and he was glad that his son-in-law was able to get him Barbasol in the green-striped can, showing that it was made with aloe.

He dabbed the shaving cream on, picked up the little plastic disposable razor, and began drawing it carefully down his cheeks. He thought the throwaway razor was one of the best things the modern world had given. He thought of how he used to fumble with dangerous double-edged blades when he loaded them into a clunky old Gillette.

He leaned close to the mirror and studied his reflection. When he was younger, his full mustache and thinning hair had made people say that he looked like Groucho Marx. He smiled, recalling that he had always answered, "Better Groucho than Harpo."

The fringe of white hair above his ears was mussed as it always was when he woke from sleep. He looked at the face in the mirror looking back at him, remembering how his daughter called what he had "male-pattern baldness," like so many men he had known over the years. Then he frowned as he thought of how both his sons developed the same pattern.

He shook the thought away and quickly finished in the bathroom, wiping away with a hand towel the few flecks of shaving cream still on his face. He combed his thin white hair, noticing its length and remarking to himself that he would soon need to have his daughter drive him to his regular barber over on Ponce de Leon Avenue.

At last it was time for him to head for the kitchen to make his breakfast. Breakfast was often the best part of his day. The fact that it never varied pleased him. He was a man of settled habits. The meal he would prepare was the same one he had eaten every morning for more than fifty years. Even when DelRee was making pancakes, French toast, or scrambled eggs for Hannah and the kids, he had stuck with his favorite routine.

It had become hard for him to stand for any length of time, so he sat on a kitchen stool near the electric range after he taken out from the refrigerator and the cabinet all that he needed to prepare the meal.

He made two egg whites poached, one piece of whole wheat bread toasted, a few prunes, and oatmeal with wheat germ sprinkled on top. It might seem like a very big breakfast to other people, but this meal would sustain him through the day until he sat down to dinner in the evening. Today would be a little easier for him since DelRee would wash his breakfast dishes.

As he sat there eating in the kitchen, he remembered Hannah bustling about in the room, cooking or baking. She had been a wonderful cook, always trying new recipes. All their friends and family had praised Hannah for her skills, not only cooking but knitting and sewing as well. She was a very creative person.

Hannah had taught DelRee to cook in her own style the kinds of food his family ate. In the end DelRee had become almost as good at cooking these as Hannah. DelRee had come to make the best chicken soup, brisket, and matzo balls you could ever eat. Sam remembered with great pleasure the rice pudding she often made. He laughed as he recalled how his daughter had often said DelRee's rice pudding was "to die for."

He heard the sound of a key going into the lock on the side kitchen door and knew it probably exactly nine o'clock. DelRee was never late. He looked up as she walked in and she said, as always, "Mornin', Mr. Sam. How you doin' today?"

Sam told her, "Doin' fine." He always told her he was feeling good. He had to because if he complained about one little twinge of pain it would get right back to his daughter, and then he would have her phoning and questioning him later in the day. But remembering how he had awakened free of his usual pains, he felt that today he truly was doing fine.

Sam and DelRee then had their morning ritual of discussing the weather. He always got a firsthand weather report from her. Today he learned it was a fine warm April morning with no chance of rain.

He knew that when she left her home it had been dark and cooler. She had to take two buses to get to his house. The city's recently built subway system did not help her at all. The nearest station was many miles from his house, way downtown on Peachtree Street near the Fox Theater. DelRee lived on the south side of Atlanta, near where life had started for him so many years ago.

Chapter Two

His breakfast was over. Sam got up to go to his room to dress. As he was going out of the kitchen, DelRee, already running water in the sink to wash up his dishes, called out, "Can I help you with anything?"

From the hallway he answered in a voice loud enough for her to hear him over the running water, "No, thank you."

In the world Sam had been raised in, it was unthinkable for a man to have a woman help bathe and dress him. One of the constant and ongoing arguments he had with his daughter was that he did not let DelRee help him more.

Sam always answered his daughter, "What? Am I feeble? Am I an invalid? I don't need a nurse."

He knew that his daughter's urging him to rely more on DelRee was part of her concern about him. He really knew that she wanted DelRee to come to the house more than three days a week. Sam knew his daughter wanted to be able to worry less about him, living alone as he did. He loved his daughter very much, and knew she loved him just as much, but they both had stubborn personalities. They would have found things to argue about no matter what.

He smiled as he recalled one of their constant battles. It was over the thermostat whenever she came to his house. If it was summer, she wanted it set sub zero. She was the same at her own house. When he went there, he made sure to take a long-sleeved sweater. It was the same in winter. She kept the temperature as low as possible.

As he took out the clothes he planned to wear, Sam thought about how his friends often had said he was a "clothes horse." It was true. He had always prided himself on being as neatly and fashionably dressed as possible. There was a very fine men's clothing store in Atlanta he shopped at for many years called Muse's. He bought everything there. In fact, he had come to know one salesman so well that the man would phone to let him know when Muse's would be having a big sale.

His daughter bought all his clothes now. It had become hard for him to go to stores and try on anything. She bought him what his granddaughter called "preppy" styles. His granddaughter was always saying Sam looked "preppy." Sam had come to know that she meant it as a compliment.

He put on a navy-blue polo shirt. His daughter had bought him many shirts of this kind. There must have been more than a dozen of them neatly folded in the drawers of the dresser he stood before. He did not like bright colors. Dark shades had always been his choice—navy, deep green, black. He told his daughter never to buy the ones with the alligator logo. For some reason he did not understand he just didn't like it.

Because it had become hard for him to do some things standing up, he sat on the bed and pulled on a well-pressed pair of khakis. Bending down with surprisingly little discomfort or pain, he put on a pair of thin black socks.

Finally, using a long-handled shoehorn, he slipped on his New Balance tennis shoes. Tennis shoes. He smiled at the name. He remembered when shoes of that sort were called plain old sneakers. That reminded him of all the Keds he had bought for the kids.

As he fastened the Velcro straps of the shoes, he had to admit how much easier they made things. His daughter had bought him shoes with the straps after she had noticed the difficulty his arthritic fingers were giving him when he was trying to tie shoelaces.

Dressed now, Sam was still feeling good. He felt compelled to go out for a walk just to prove to himself that he still could. DelRee had told him the weather was nice, and he had no deadlines to meet or anything pressing at all, so why not?

He went to the dresser top, put on the Seiko watch his son Cary had given him, put his wallet in his back pocket, and was reaching toward the pewter plate where kept small change and his house key when he was distracted by DelRee's voice saying, "What are you doin', Mr. Sam?"

He turned at the sound of her voice and stepped out of his room. She was standing in the kitchen doorway, still holding the breakfast bowl she was drying.

Sam said, "I'm getting ready to go for a walk just like the good old days."

DelRee said, "Oh, no. Not another walk like the long ones you used to take?"

Sam smiled as he said, "Yep. I feel too good to stay cooped up all day. You finish and leave early, DelRee. Go home and play with your grandkids."

DelRee had a pained expression on her face. "Now, Mr. Sam, don't you go pushin' yourself too hard. You ain't gettin' any younger."

Sam smiled and said, "Who is? I'm taking a walk and I'll be out of the house a long time. And don't you go getting on the phone to my daughter, you hear? If she knew I was out walking she'd call the cops to pick me up and bring me home."

As if to show DelRee how good he felt, he moved more quickly than usual on his cane to the tall antique coat rack Hannah had bought years ago. He smiled remembering how Hannah had said, "It was made for that spot by the door."

He pulled on a light tan cardigan sweater, knowing how April weather could change in Atlanta. Then he took down his cap, put it on, and was out the door before DelRee could say another word.

Chapter Three

Out of the house, Sam moved quickly down the three steps from his porch, across some flagstones set in the lawn to the driveway, and then up to the sidewalk on St. Charles Place.

He paused near the mailbox and, as he always did, looked back at the house that meant so much to him, calling up as it did so many memories. It was hard to get across to his daughter how much it meant to him to keep living in the house, a house he had known from a time before she was even born.

It was a house that Hannah had fallen in love with years before they had come to live in it themselves. They had come to many dinners and parties at the house when it was owned by Joe and Selma Levin. Hannah, who loved everything having to do with the arts, had become very close to Selma, who was a painter good enough to have some of her paintings owned by the High Museum.

Joe was in the liquor business. Back then the law was—maybe still is for all he knew, Sam thought—that the owner of a liquor store had to live in the same county where his store was located. Joe had just bought a business in DeKalb County and had to move.

Knowing how much he and Hannah loved the place and their need, with three small children, to move from an apartment, Joe offered to sell it to Sam at a very fair price. Joe even helped Sam arrange a mortgage at a very good rate through his bank. Twenty thousand dollars was a lot of money in 1949. "Still is," Sam said to himself. Sam missed Joe and Selma, who like so many of his friends and family had passed away.

It always amazed Sam how memories of his life, good and bad, filled his mind whenever he took a walk. It was 1995 and he was still here. Eighty-eight years old and most of his immediate family was gone, except for his sister Marie who was two years younger than he and still going strong.

Sam felt sad thinking of the fact that so many people he had known and loved had died, but he was especially grieved by the loss of Hannah, his wife of sixty-one years, and his two boys. Although they were grown men at the time of their deaths, Sam would always think of them as his boys.

Now the Robkin family came down basically to him and Marie, and his daughter, of course. The baby. He had to laugh—some "baby." Fifty-two years old. At least, he thought, he was not completely alone. His daughter and her husband had always been and still were there for him.

Sam felt truly sorry for his daughter, losing her brothers at so early an age. They should all have grown old together and had one another for strength and support. Now all she had from her original family was him and Marie. Sam knew that he had become his daughter's constant concern and source of worry. He saw her at least twice a week and talked on the phone with her every day. Almost every conversation they had boiled down to one thing and one thing only: she wanted him to sell the house and come live with her and her husband.

She had an answer every time Sam gave a reason why he wanted to stay, even alone, in the house he loved. He never told her his deepest fear, that moving out and losing his freedom would be the final signal of his losing the fight to old age. No matter what he said, she countered with truths that he sensed, but could never agree to. Her own kids were grown and out on their own. She had plenty of room. She could cook his meals, do his laundry and so on, over and over.

Sam knew that underneath it all was her deep concern that by living with her he would not be alone. He knew that she feared something would happen and she would not be there to help. No matter how many times he told her he didn't mind living alone, that he was careful and still capable of taking care of himself, she had an answer to shoot back at him. It had become an obsession with her, worrying about his living alone.

A good example of her persistence was the device he wore on a cord around his neck. If he fell or required any help in an emergency, a push of its button would make a phone call to a monitored center that would send the needed assistance. Even though he had fought hard to resist wearing the device, she had finally worn him down and won.

Of course, she immediately began a new campaign. Since the device worked only when he was at home, she wanted to get him a cell phone to have with him the few times he left the house.

At the moment he seemed to be winning the battle against getting such a phone, mainly by pointing out how rarely he was ever alone outside the house.

He had all but promised never to do the very thing he was doing now, leaving the house for a long walk alone. But Sam knew his daughter was far from giving up.

Sam had told her, "If I keel over in the street, God forbid, someone will be there to help me."

His daughter had said she would like to believe that, but the world had become more and more filled with mean and harmful people. Even Atlanta had more than its share of them. Sam read the paper every day and watched the evening news on television. He was very aware of how high the crime rate had grown in the city and its suburbs. Even the worst criminal act of all, murder, had reached out and come into his family.

Looking around the street he had lived on for so many years, Sam thought how peaceful and quiet the neighborhood seemed. It made him think how the whole city had seemed so when he was growing up on the south side.

Chapter Four

Thinking about his childhood on the south side brought up memories of the person in his life who dominated those days, his mother, Annie Rosenbloom Robkin. Most of the memories he had, he sadly admitted, weren't good, especially near the end of her life. He smiled as he realized that his daughter's efforts to get him to move reminded him how hard he had worked to get Annie to admit that she needed assistance. She was truly an ill-tempered woman.

Ill-tempered? She was a downright pain in the ass. Today she would certainly be called a "drama queen." It was an expression he had picked up somewhere—probably television—and it had stuck with him since it completely fit his mother's personality.

After he had persuaded Annie finally to accept living at the Jewish Home on 14th Street, he had thought his troubles were over, but no. He wished he had a dollar for every time he had been called by the director to come in to see what he could do to help straighten out the troubles the staff was having with her.

She'd had so many roommates. She drove off at least half a dozen before she finally was given a room all to herself. She was probably the only person in the history of the old place to live without a roommate.

But she was even worse when it came to the food being served. She complained so much and so loudly that the director gave up and let her work in the kitchen. Annie was, the director had to admit, a wonderful cook, and in the time she worked with the kitchen staff everyone had to admit how much better the meals had become.

Whatever bad memories Sam had of Annie, he had to admit she had been very good about letting him and Marie have a lot of freedom when they were kids. The part of Atlanta where he grew up was greatly changed, but back then it had been a tight neighborhood, a place of many small houses crowded together, filled with families who knew each other. The fathers went to work and the mothers stayed home all day and kept an eye on one another's children.

Looking back, he realized how safe the old neighborhood had been. He and Marie usually would spend almost all day either playing in the streets or spending time in the houses of other kids. He wondered if children growing up today could have the same sense of security he had grown up with.

When it came to his mother Sam had practically no real emotion. Still, she had let Marie and him roam. He had to give Annie credit for that. He had been thinking a lot lately of his mother and father and the only grandparent he had known. Sam's daughter had recently been talking with him a whole lot about his past. She'd even got a shoebox of old pictures from Marie, old fading photographs that stirred memories of people and places he had not thought about for years.

Sam had started his walk at a very brisk pace when he first came out of the house, hurrying to get away from DelRee's not wanting him to push himself. Now he was two houses up and out of sight of his own house where he knew DelRee was watching, and probably reaching for the telephone to call his daughter. He slowed his pace considerably. Back when his walks were exercises aimed at controlling his weight, he moved along at a very fast and regular speed, but today he just wanted to take a plain old steady stroll.

By now he was nearing the end of his block where his street ended at Highland Avenue, the main road through the area. He planned to go a good ways along Highland before turning back. So far he was feeling good. Slow as he was walking, he began to feel confident that everything was going to work out well.

Sam heard a dog barking inside the last house on St. Charles. The sound of the dog reminded him of another good thing he could say about his mother: she had allowed him and Marie to have pets.

Of course, Annie had a reason she let her kids have pets. At the time she and his father were running a small grocery store on Powell Street in the section of Atlanta known as Cabbagetown. Annie figured the cats and dogs would keep rats and mice away from the store. As usual she was right. Sam remembered his favorite dog, a terrier that he called simply Pup. Pup was the champion rat killer.

Thinking about Pup reminded him of his father's real love of animals. As mean as Annie was, Abe Robkin was exactly the opposite. Where she was loud, Abe was quiet. Where she was agitated, Abe was calm. The animals seemed to sense that and stayed close to him.

Sam laughed. One year Abe kept a goat in the back-yard. Abe and a man who worked at the store built a small cart that the goat would pull, giving the kids in the neighborhood rides. An old photo Marie had given to his daughter showed Sam sitting proudly in that little cart. Sam chuckled, remembering that he had named the goat Billy. A goat named Billy and a dog named Pup. "Not very original, Sam," he murmured.

By now Sam had reached the corner of St. Charles and Highland Avenue. Looking ahead, he saw how heavy the traffic was on the cross street. He could see cars and delivery trucks going by in a steady stream in both directions.

Seeing all the traffic on Highland reminded him of how much he missed driving. His daughter and son-in-law had convinced him six years before that he had to give up driving, not because he was a bad driver—though he had to admit that his reflexes had slowed—but because there were just too many cars with what his daughter called "crazy" drivers. Noticing how fast people drove on Highland, narrow as it was with cars parked on both sides, brought a memory of some close calls he'd had. His daughter was right. People drove too fast and there were too many cars at all hours of the day. It seemed that every minute of the day was a rush hour in Atlanta.

One good thing that came about from his having to stop driving was that he had been able to do something nice for DelRee. One of her sons was graduating from high school and she had told Sam how much the boy wanted a car of his own. Sam said, "Take mine and give it to him." He'd meant for her to take it free, but she insisted on paying him something. "Okay," he had answered. "A hundred bucks spread out over a year."

Even though the car was more than five years old, Sam had maintained it religiously and it was in very good shape. Every so often he would see it pull into his driveway when DelRee's son drove her to work on days when the weather was too bad for her to be standing around at bus stops.

Giving up driving Sam knew was the first sign of independence getting away from him. It was at that time that he really began to take seriously his daily walking. He knew that he had to keep going. He had decided to push himself as long as he could. What was the old saying? "If you don't use it, you lose it." Long walks gave Sam a sense of independence at least partially regained. It was why getting out of the house this day was so important.

He turned to the right onto the sidewalk on Highland Avenue, and glanced at the little park the city had made of the small plot of land where a one-story library had stood for years, the library his kids had used, especially his daughter. When the county built a big new library over on Ponce de Leon, they tore down the old one and made the park.

Looking to his left, Sam saw across the street the building that had housed the neighborhood's main supermarket. It had gone the way of the library, replaced by new and bigger stores over on Ponce, but it had not been torn down. Now the old building had been divided and contained shops and restaurants.

Across St. Charles from the old Colonial Store building was what had been the neighborhood drug store. Not a Walgreens or Eckerds but a privately owned business. Dr. Shackleford was the pharmacist who had owned it. He was an extremely nice and gentle man who had worked past retirement age for as long as he could. When his health got bad, his son had taken it over and kept it going for many years.

Like most of the old drug stores, Dr. Shackleford's had a beautiful black-and-white marble soda fountain with a row of stools in front of it. Kids would stop in and fill up the stools when the school bus let them off. They would get cherry Cokes and ice cream sundaes and snacks of all kinds. His daughter said they had the best egg salad sandwich in all of Atlanta.

Back then the world was so different that Dr. Shackleford would let the kids run tabs if they didn't have money to pay that afternoon. When their parents came into the store, Dr. Shackleford would collect and clear the tabs. The world was really simpler then. People didn't fax or email their prescriptions in to be filled. They carried them to the store in person.

Sam knew that things were completely different these days. Faxing and e-mailing and having a computer in your house and what was the other thing? Oh yes, the Internet. All of that had come along too late for him. His daughter had tried more than once to explain all the marvelous things that were taking place, but Sam said he was just too old to get very involved in this new technology. The discussions had reminded him of all the wonderful things he had seen develop in his lifetime—movies, radio, then television, and an invention that he especially loved, the microwave oven. "Who knows," he almost said aloud, "what inventions are coming along for the young people of today?"

Still looking to his left at the row of stores across Highland Avenue, he saw that they were no longer the kinds of businesses he remembered. He recalled that the shop next to the drugstore had been the neighborhood's dry cleaners. How many hundreds of times had he gone into that shop with Hannah's dresses or the suits he wore making his sales calls? He knew it was important to look neat and well-pressed when he called on customers, and he always had.

Years ago, next to the dry cleaners had been a wonderful ice cream parlor—not part of any chain but a privately owned business. Over the years it had been successful enough to have a plant in the rear of the building where they made all different flavors of ice cream that they sold to local stores. Sam read a big sign over the place's show window and learned that the place was now selling modern furniture. Another change. He had seen so many. Still, he hoped to see more.

Chapter Five

Sam was walking much slower than he had back when he was younger. "Younger," he muttered, with a little laugh. "Younger was sixty." Still, though he now depended more on his cane than he had in the past, he was moving along steadily. So far his knees were not troubling him. Maybe the shots the doctor had given him the other day were still working.

The side of Highland Avenue he was on had few businesses. The area was mostly residential. There were small plots with bungalow-type houses and an occasional two or three-story building that Sam guessed had been turned into apartments. Off to the right among all the houses he took notice of the snowy white branches of dogwood trees. Atlanta in April was full of flowering trees of all kinds but mostly dogwoods. It started Sam's mind recalling the years he had lived up in New York. How different Atlanta was from all the brick and pavement and tall tenements of Manhattan and Queens and Brooklyn.

Some months after Sam's bar mitzvah, his mother Annie got the wild idea that the Robkin family should move up to the big city. Sam never knew for sure what gave her the crazy notion that they would make their fortune there. Still she pushed and pushed and made life miserable for Abe until he finally agreed to make the move. Nobody, not even Abe, could stand up to Annie's constant arguing and nagging. Abe sold the house and store on Powell Street. The money from the sales paid for the move up North. Annie even talked her younger sister Mary and her husband into moving at the same time.

In the long run, like most of Annie's schemes, the whole thing was a flop, and after a few years the Robkins were back in Atlanta. Sam had to admit, though, one wonderfully good thing had come out of those New York years. If he had not been living up there he would never have met Hannah and had all the happy years with her.

But before he met Hannah, Sam had to get through some rough times. He hated going to school, not because he was not a good student but because all the other kids, all tough little New Yorkers, bullied him and made fun of his Southern accent. Finally, when he was sixteen, he told his mother he was quitting school.

"Good," Annie said. "Now you can get a job and help us out with the money you make." Annie was always lamenting that they never had enough to live on.

And that's what he did. He got a job in a grocery store stocking shelves and sweeping up, but the little bit of money that he was able to turn over to her each week must not have been enough. One day he came up from work to the apartment and found his clothes and other things all bundled in a heap. Annie told him he would have to find somewhere else to live. It turned out that she had rented his room to a boarder and what the man paid in rent was much more than Sam's contribution.

Luckily, his Aunt Mary, who was as sweet and gentle as Annie was bitter and harsh, took Sam in. Mary and her husband were far from wealthy and their two-room apartment was small, but they made a home for Sam. Thinking of Mary's kindness gave Sam a little rush of emotion. He loved her. As for his mother, he had not a single good feeling.

Sam was walking very slowly now, but not from discomfort or pain. All the thoughts he was thinking about his New York years were filling his memory and causing him to go slower. He guessed that being out and about for the first time in months was such a change that it had made him start to think about things that had not thought of for years.

He looked back across Highland Avenue to the buildings he was now opposite. He saw that he was parallel with the old Highland Theater, once a movie house where all the local kids would go on Saturday mornings and stay almost all day. Back then there were cartoons and serials and even double feature shows. His daughter had told him that she and her friends from school would sneak in hamburgers from the Majestic Diner over on Ponce de Leon to eat while they watched the movies. They also sneaked in all kinds of sweets from a shop called The Candy Pan that was a few doors down from the Majestic.

And now, instead of displaying the current movies or coming attractions, the Highland Theater's marquee read "Atlanta Metropolitan Church." His daughter had told Sam that the theater had been converted to a non-sectarian place of worship for men and women who were now being called "gay." Many such people had bought houses and were now living in the neighborhood.

Having gay people living nearby didn't bother Sam at all. He was not judgmental, though he had trouble understanding what was in them to make them so different from men like himself. He had seen many TV shows—some fiction, some documentaries—about homosexuality, but never any show that explained it in a way he could understand. Live and let live was Sam's attitude.

His daughter had pointed out to him that gay people buying houses in the area was a very good thing. Their houses—many of them extensively remodeled—were usually well-maintained and had what real estate people called curb appeal, and kept the local property values high.

Sam had to agree with her. He'd had trouble believing when he had learned that houses near where he lived, some of them not even as big as his own, were selling for more than two-hundred thousand dollars.

Sam was kept aware of what his daughter had told him about rising property values by being pestered almost daily by real estate people constantly calling him to see if he was interested in selling his own house. He had wondered how they knew so much about him. He could understand how they got his telephone number as it was the same one he'd been listed under for thirty years, but the callers always seemed to know more about him than they should have— things like his being a widower living alone and how long he had owned the house. His daughter explained that it was the Internet. Again with the Internet. She said you could get all kinds of information from the Internet.

Chapter Six

By now Sam was passing a building that had once been a delicatessen. He smiled, thinking about all the Sunday mornings when he had walked there to buy lox and bagels that had been shipped down from New York. Back then there wasn't anyone in Atlanta who baked bagels.

If any friends of theirs were making a trip to New York, Hannah would ask them to bring back bagels. She would freeze dozens of them. All her life her favorite food had been whitefish on a bagel with onions and tomato slices. Hannah was a true New Yorker. After all, she had been born and raised in Brooklyn. Seeing the building where he had bought bagels and how Hannah loved them stirred thoughts of his wife.

He thought of how difficult her childhood had been, so difficult that she never talked about it. Her father was killed in a terrible accident, crushed against a wall by an out-of-control taxi. Her mother died soon after. For some reason he never knew, Hannah and her younger sister had been given to her elderly grandmother, her mother's mother, to be raised.

The old lady spoke only Yiddish and was really hard and strict with the girls. Hannah never spoke a word about those days. It was, he figured, too painful a time.

Kids went to work young in those days. In her early teens Hannah got a job in a ladies dress and coat factory located in Manhattan. By the time she was sixteen or seventeen, Hannah had become a beauty and was given the job of modeling the company's dresses and coats for buyers.

Every morning she would leave her grandmother's apartment and in the subway station's ladies room change her clothes and put on her makeup. She kept the old lady in the dark about her being a model. It was easier to let her grandmother think she ran a sewing machine all day.

Sam chuckled as he thought that if he had not let his friend Julius talk him into going to a dance at the YMHA he would never have met Hannah and how his life would have been completely different.

Sam stopped walking for a moment when the thought of Julius Silverman entered his mind. He felt a pang of regret for having lost touch with the best friend of his younger years.

While he was still living with his Aunt Mary, Sam was always looking to improve his situation and kept getting better and better jobs. The increasing rent money he gave his Aunt Mary must have infuriated his mother. He hoped she regretted putting him out of his family's apartment. Probably not. Annie never regretted anything.

It was when he was working at a wholesale materials company that he first met Julius. They hit it off together right away and became close as brothers, the best of friends. Julius had even been his best man when he married Hannah a few years later.

Julius was from The Bronx and at the time was still living with his parents. He and Julius planned to get an apartment together when they both had saved enough money. They did manage to go in together and buy an old used Ford that they shared, driving it all over Manhattan and even out to Coney Island.

They often double-dated. Julius had a way with the girls and helped Sam get over his shyness. Sam's Southern accent intrigued the girls they met. What had been a problem in his school days later became a real positive.

One morning Sam came to work late once too often at the wholesale company and the boss fired him. Julius got mad and in protest quit. Sam always thought when he remembered that day what a great friend Julius was. The thought of the loyalty and friendship Julius showed by quitting stirred Sam's heart.

When he and Hannah moved back to Atlanta in the thirties, Sam lost contact with Julius and his wife Marcella. In Atlanta Sam had gone to work for an uncle who was starting to build a small chain of grocery stores. Sam worked hard and came to learn the food business which became his life's work. Being so busy at work and having to support his growing family made it hard for Sam to keep up with Julius and Marcella.

Standing still for a moment on Highland Avenue, Sam thought how wrong it had been of him to fail to keep alive his friendship with Julius. He even wondered if Julius was still alive. He hoped so. Sam promised himself to ask his daughter to try to find Julius. Maybe she could use the Internet. Still thinking about Julius, Sam sighed and started walking again.

As Sam's mind came out of his memories of his years in New York, he saw that he was now passing the steep steps up to the doors of the biggest building in the neighborhood, the big brick Baptist church. Surprised, he became aware of how far he had walked already. He was close to Virginia Avenue, the destination he'd thought of as his halfway point. He also sensed that he was beginning to feel a little tired, and he even felt a slight twinge of pain in his right knee. "Bone on bone" the doctor had said of his old knees. "Tired or not," Sam told himself, "I'm going to go on. With God's help, I'll make it all the way and get back home."

The challenge to himself excited him, though he felt sad as he thought how a walk like this one when he was younger would not have bothered him, would not have winded him even a little. He wanted so badly to be able still to do all the things he once did with such ease. Up ahead and very close now was the intersection of Virginia and Highland Avenues. He told himself that when he crossed Virginia he would sit and rest on the bus stop's bench on the other side in front of what had once been an Esso gas station and was now some kind of a small convenience store. If he sat for a while, he could gather his strength for the walk back to St. Charles Place and home.

Waiting for the traffic light to change so that he could cross the intersection, he recalled that this very place, where Highland crossed Virginia, was what people meant when they spoke of "The Highlands." Where those two streets met was the center of it all, the whole changed neighborhood. Now Virginia and Highland had become a spot that people came to from all over Atlanta and the suburbs. Even visitors from other cities had learned of it and made it part of their Atlanta experience. People came there to stroll up and down and to browse in the old stores and shops, converted into what his daughter called trendy boutiques. New attractive restaurants and bars gave patrons pleasant places to eat and drink. Sam shook his head slightly as he recalled how ordinary a place it had been in years past.

The intersection of Virginia and Highland was where he and others in the neighborhood had come to buy groceries and do other common errands like getting haircuts, getting shoes mended, and getting clothes dry-cleaned. It had been just a couple of streets full of busy merchants. Now it had become like one of the malls, Phipps Plaza or Lenox Square.

Once when his daughter had been driving him to a doctor's appointment, they had passed what had been a vacant lot near the firehouse farther down Highland and she had pointed out a new building there. It had stores in it called The Gap and Pier 1. The names made no sense to him. What could they be selling?

The traffic light changed, and Sam slowly made his way to the bench he was heading for and sat on the far corner. When he reached it he saw that there was an advertisement on the bench's back for a law firm, one he often saw in commercials during the newscast he watched every night at six. Another change, Sam thought. In the world Sam remembered, lawyers and doctors did not need to advertise.

As he slowly lowered himself to sit on the bench, he gave a little sigh, only partly because he was at last getting some rest, but he knew he was sighing because the lawyer's ad had started him thinking sadly of his oldest child Alan who had himself been a lawyer. Alan was found dead of a heart attack in his early forties. Given the way Alan lived, his death was a shock but not really a surprise.

Alan was a bright boy. He had worked hard and put himself through Woodrow Wilson Law School at night. He opened a practice in Buckhead and did very well, doing legal work for the friends he had made at Grady High School and their families. He was making very good money, Sam remembered, but maybe that was what led to his early death.

Sam wondered how Alan could have ever had a normally long life with the habits and lifestyle he had. He had become morbidly overweight and was a huge gambler. A confirmed bachelor, his good earnings supported his ways of gambling and overindulgence. Sam figured Alan had probably lost at least a million dollars in his short lifetime. He had made trips to Las Vegas so many times Sam lost count.

Alan had two close friends who were brothers and who were almost always at his son's apartment. One had been left by his wife. He was a gourmet cook and was always preparing extravagant meals. The other had no wife or girlfriend, and Sam's daughter had told him that this friend's interest in women was questionable among many people and made them wonder. The three of them had traveled all around the United States and Europe to dine extravagantly at restaurants run by four-star chefs. Alan led his life in a large, freewheeling way, and the brothers were happy to tag along with him.

Sam's daughter had told him that she had always felt the brothers were a very bad influence on Alan. Not only were they always at Alan's apartment, but when his daughter and female friends of hers came to visit, they were extremely rude. She figured that the brothers just did not like women. They were the type of men who tried to make women feel bad about themselves and took every opportunity to do so. Of course, they were entirely different when they were around Sam, always friendly and joking. Sam liked them. He had no reason not to.

The early deaths of his two sons were the greatest shocks of Sam's life. He had heard or read somewhere that to lose a child is like having your own breath sucked out of you, a hollowing out. Unfortunately, he had come to know that this was indeed true.

But as hard as it had been for him, seeing Hannah's reaction to the tragedies had been ever harder. She turned totally inward, never talking about the deaths, in fact almost never talking at all. This vital, funny, intelligent woman just closed herself up and never came out of the shell she had made.

Sam remembered the day he and his daughter had to admit her to the Jewish Home. His daughter's eyes were full of tears as they did so. Hannah was angry, as they knew she would be, but it had to be done. There were too many medical problems and she had fallen a number of times.

Sam had taken care of her for a long time. Everyone told him what a good job he had done, but the time had come. It was truly a heartbreaking moment for him when she was taken to a room. Sam knew she had to have professional help, and so she did up until the day she died.

So now it had come down to just him and his daughter. Sam knew he had become her constant concern and worry. He saw her at least twice a week and talked to her on the phone every day, and in almost every conversation she would ask him to please, *please* sell the house and come live with her and her husband.

Sam told her over and over that he was perfectly happy living alone, but she had become obsessed with the idea of getting him to move in with her, not realizing that where he lived and the way he lived gave him a feeling of certainty. If he could keep on resisting her then he could stay in the surroundings that he was sure of, and that meant so much to him. All of it: the neighborhood he knew so well and the house itself, filled with memories of Hannah, friends, and especially of his children growing up there.

Even though the bench he was sitting on had given Sam the period of rest that he knew he needed, he looked at his watch and saw that it was almost eleven. He would have to start moving soon.

The day had grown considerably warmer. Maybe, he thought, wearing the cardigan, light though it was, hadn't been such a good idea. He knew he would have to keep it on, though. He couldn't carry it and handle his cane at the same time.

Sitting in the warm April sun— not scorching as it would be in a couple of months—was, he had to admit, pleasant. It made him think of the many days he and Marie as kids had spent down in Fayetteville with their grandfather, Zaidie Rosenbloom. Sam closed his eyes and found himself remembering those days.

Chapter Seven

Every summer when school was out, Abe would drive Sam and Marie to stay for a month or more with Annie's father, Avram Rosenbloom, who owned a successful dry goods store on the square near the courthouse in Fayetteville. The town is only twenty or so miles south of Atlanta, but in those days, with no expressways, it was not a simple trip.

Years later Sam marveled when he thought of Zaidie, the Yiddish word for grandfather. How brave Avram must have been to have left the troubled world of Russia in the late nineteenth century with a wife and three daughters. (Aunt Mary, his youngest daughter, was born in the U.S.) For years he traveled with a horse and cart in middle Georgia, selling clothes and household items to the country people. Eventually he saved enough to start a store and buy a farmhouse outside the town. Sam never knew Jennie, Zaidie's wife. She died in 1911, when Sam was four years old. Zaidie was a pious man. He was one of the founders of Atlanta's first synagogue. Once a week he would drive a horse and cart the forty-mile round trip to buy kosher food in Atlanta.

The first thing Zaidie did when Abe dropped them off was take Sam and Marie to his store and fit each of them with a pair of overalls and a shirt. From the time they came to Fayetteville till they went home, they did not wear shoes.

They stayed at the farmhouse with a well that was down the road from Zaidie's store. He always had a couple of stray dogs and cats he was feeding. Sam and his sister played all day. Zaidie put no restrictions on them.

Sitting in the warm sun, Sam could sense how easy it would be to fall asleep. That reminded him of his principal recollection of his summer days in Fayetteville. Each day he and Marie would go to Zaidie's store and have lunch. After lunch Zaidie would go across the road to the courthouse lawn. He'd lie down and take a nap. This rest after a meal was a habit carried over from the old country. He left his two women clerks in charge of the store. Over the years everyone in the town came to know Mr. Rosenbloom and had become used to seeing him lying down asleep on the grass in the shade of an old oak tree.

Zaidie always left strict orders that if he was not back at the store in an hour for someone to come and wake him. Sam and Marie loved it when he over-slept and they were sent to wake him. They would tickle his arm or his nose with a long blade of grass and he would pop up sputtering and spouting Yiddish. When he was fully awake he would laugh along with them.

Sam opened his eyes, blinking in the sunlight, and thought he had better not fall asleep. There was nobody around to tickle him awake.

Leaning forward on the bench, his crossed hands resting on top of his cane, he looked up and saw the street sign that read Virginia Avenue. It made him think of all the times he had driven up Highland heading for this very intersection. Sometimes he turned left, sometimes right.

If he turned left he would arrive at Henry Grady High School. He remembered that it was once known as Boys High. He smiled as he thought of how often he had driven his kids to football games at the stadium on the school's grounds. He would drop them off and wait until they disappeared into the crowd of other students milling around. The field's light towers would be on in the dusk, and he could hear the band playing somewhere inside the stadium. It was not great music but it was loud. That was what the kids wanted—noise and lights and a feeling of excitement. Once upon a time, so did he.

Eventually the boys reached driving age and they would go to the games on their own with friends, but for a few years after that Sam drove his daughter and some of her friends to those Friday night games. When he picked them up later when the game ended, they always asked, "Can we go to the Varsity?"

The Varsity was, and still is, an Atlanta landmark downtown near Georgia Tech. Sam knew but could hardly believe the place was still in business, and not only there; from his daughter he had learned that they had opened a couple of locations in the suburbs. The original establishment downtown was said to be the largest drive-in in all of the Unites States, selling more Coca-Colas at one time than any other place in the world. Who knows, Sam thought, maybe that was still true.

All the kids loved to go to the Varsity. The place was famous for chili dogs, hamburgers, onion rings, and fried pies, all of it served hot and fast.

Thinking of the kind of food served there almost made Sam's stomach gurgle. He had never eaten a thing from the Varsity and never would. He had suffered from a pyloric ulcer from his teen years on and had always stuck to a strict diet of fairly bland food.

One of the features of the Varsity that the kids loved was that when you drove in—back then all the cars had chrome bumpers—one of the many young black men who worked as carhops taking orders would jump on and ride while you looked for a place to park. They each had a number assigned, and the one who hopped on your bumper would put a card with his number on your windshield so that the others would know your car was taken.

All of the carhops had little shticks they performed. One chanted a sort of poetry, the kind that kids today called rap. Some of the others sang and a few did little dances as they went away with your order. Of course, they were all vying for the biggest tip possible since they made their livings on tips alone.

Sam smiled as he remembered that when his younger son Cary came home from New York to visit, the first place he wanted to go was to the Varsity. Always.

Only a week or so before, Sam's daughter had told him that she and her friend Arlene had gone to the Varsity recently for lunch and it had been great. Grown women, the two of them. Some things from your youth just stay with you.

He had been pleased when his daughter mentioned Arlene, her friend for thirty years or more. Many times in the past when his daughter had been working,

Arlene had helped her out by taking Sam to doctors' appointments. He had come to love being with her. She was a cheerful, witty woman. It didn't hurt that she was extremely attractive. Old as he had become, Sam still appreciated good-looking women.

Thinking of his many drives down Virginia Avenue to Grady High School made Sam remember one ride in particular, one that would always remain strong in his memory. It was back in 1961 when his daughter was just going into twelfth grade. She usually rode in a carpool, but Sam made sure that he drove her to school that day.

The time had come for segregation to end. That day the schools were going to be integrated and Grady had been chosen to be one of the first. Sam had been raised in an era when the races were kept apart all over the South, and he was sorry to remember that he had become used to the idea. Hannah, raised in New York, had always hated segregation and was happy to see it coming to an end.

His daughter's class was chosen to be the actual one that two black kids—a boy and a girl—were to join. Sam remembered the long line of cars he was in as he went up 8th Street and turned right on Charles Allen Drive where the front of the school was.

There were police cars from both Fulton County and the City of Atlanta, as well as the Georgia State

Patrol and news trucks from the television stations. Up and down the street a large crowd of people milled around. As Sam's car was idling in a line near the school's entrance, a state trooper came up to Sam's window, looked in, and saw that Sam's daughter was a student. The trooper said it would be only a few more minutes before she could get out. Sam nodded and thanked him.

A few minutes later another officer came up, opened the door for his daughter, and escorted her to the school steps. Sam was proud of his daughter, seeing how calmly and bravely she accepted the situation. He watched as his daughter joined the line of her classmates. All the kids were, like his daughter, being quiet and orderly. He knew all these kids came from good homes and had been raised with good values, knowing right from wrong. They accepted change. Young people were always better at accepting change.

As Sam drove away that day he took notice of the crowd of grown-ups gathered near the school. The people appeared calm. There was no one making a scene, no shouting of taunts and racial slurs, no screaming of obscenities like the mobs in other southern cities he had seen on the television news. Good for Atlanta, he thought.

Still, the whole experience had shaken Sam. In the days and weeks of that summer before the first day of school there had been a lot of meetings of families who lived in the neighborhood. Some of the parents were truly fearful, afraid of repercussions, maybe even violence. A few of them spoke of taking their kids out of Grady and sending them to one or the other of two private schools. Being private institutions, those schools at that time were not bound by law to integrate. Both schools had excellent reputations. Sam was happy when his daughter said she didn't want to go anywhere but Grady. Her brothers had gone there, and she had many, many friends there and didn't want to leave those friends.

Her decision pleased him and Hannah. It showed she had good sense and knew integration was the right thing. But Sam and Hannah were pleased also because the tuition at one of those private schools would have placed a heavy burden on them, not to mention the difficulty they would have in seeing to it that his daughter got to school on time each day. Both of the schools were on the other side of the city and he would have had to find a way for his daughter to be there early in the morning.

Sam always suspected that his daughter had thought of all the troubles he and Hannah would have had if she had transferred and that she had consciously spared them the hardships. She was thoughtful and considerate of others, even as a teenager. And stubborn as a mule, with a mind of her own, even then.

Chapter Eight

Still sitting on the bench at the corner of Highland and Virginia, Sam felt his mind turn to thinking of the many times he had gone the other way, turning right off Highland and heading into the leafy, quiet streets. A few blocks up was one street he would never forget—Rosedale, just off Virginia. The street was narrow and had cars parked on both sides. It was always hard to find a place for his car when he visited. The block of Rosedale he remembered had a number of apartment buildings built back in the 1920s.

One building stood out in his memory because it was there that his three aunts lived. They were his mother's sisters, the Rosenbloom girls—Lottie, Sara, and Mary. Two were widows. Each sister had her own separate apartment.

It was a U-shaped building with two apartments up and two down. Each apartment had a tiny porch overlooking a three-sided courtyard. Sam drove there often as a grown man to visit his Aunt Mary who had been so kind to him when he was just a kid in New York. Mary lived in the first group on the lower left. Directly across the courtyard on the lower right was Aunt Lottie, the eldest. On the bend of the horseshoe on the bottom floor was Aunt Sara.

Whenever Sam came to visit, either alone or with Hannah and one or all of the kids, he actually tried to sneak in as he headed for Aunt Mary's back door so that Aunt Lottie would not know he was there, but damned if nearly every time he came Aunt Lottie would show up on her porch and holler, "Yoo hoo! Hello, Sammy!" He would always call back a warm greeting, but never crossed over to go to her apartment.

Sam had never been very fond of Aunt Lottie. He remembered in fact how as a kid she had terrified him. She was a tiny woman, five foot tall or so, maybe less, and she weighed about ninety-five pounds. Little as she was, she was still scary. She had a terrible, volatile temper and cursed worse than any man when she got mad.

When Sam was a boy, he would sometimes be sent on some errand or other by his mother to the large dry goods store Lottie and her husband owned on Marietta Street in downtown Atlanta. Today the store would be considered a small department store.

They sold all kinds of things, from packets of sewing needles up to full-size iceboxes.

Once when Sam was maybe eight or nine, he was playing in the back of the store with Lottie's son Buddy who was a year or so younger than Sam. Suddenly Lottie showed up. She was mad at Buddy for something. She started chasing Buddy. When they were near the open door that led to the basement steps, Lottie had caught up with Buddy and was reaching to grab him by the collar when they both went tumbling headfirst down the steps. What amazed Sam was that neither of them was seriously hurt. When they came back up the steps, she started chasing Buddy all over again. Sam remembered it all after nearly eighty years as if it had happened yesterday.

Sam had told his daughter many Aunt Lottie stories that he had heard from the other sisters, but there was one he could tell because he saw with his own eyes.

Now Lottie's husband was a sweet, quiet man who adored her, mean spirit and all. One day Sam was at the store when Lottie got mad at her husband for something, probably for selling a colored man a loaf of bread for a nickel instead of ten cents. Lottie took a Coca-Cola bottle—one of the old thick green glass ones—and threw it all the way across the store. It hit him in the chest and nearly knocked him over. Sam always laughed when he told the story. If that bottle had hit him in the head, he could have been killed.

His daughter had trouble believing that little shriveled old woman she remembered could have been so mean and nasty-tempered. "And threw like a shortstop," Sam said with another laugh.

Aunt Sara was the aunt he had been around the least when he was young. She had married a man from the Tidewater in Virginia and gone up there to live with him. He wasn't an eye doctor, but he'd been trained somehow to fit people for eyeglasses. He had taught Sara the trade and they both traveled all around the region, mostly to small rural towns, giving vision tests and selling glasses.

When Sara's husband died, he had not left her very well off. She moved back to Atlanta to be near her father and sisters. Sara had a happy, vibrant personality. She loved to read and worked at educating herself. Sam often brought her books from the library at St. Charles and Highland.

One subject really interested Sara because she remembered how it had troubled the Jewish community in Atlanta when she was young. She had Sam bring here everything he could find about the Leo Frank case.

Leo Frank was the manager of The National Pencil Company, later to become Scripto. He had come to Atlanta from New York and eventually married into the Selig family. He was active in the synagogue and even became the first president of B'nai Brith of Atlanta.

In 1913 he was accused of raping and murdering a thirteen-year old girl who worked at the factory, a girl named Mary Phagan. There was a long trial, marred by much anti-Semitism. That Leo was a Jew from Brooklyn and (by those day's standards) a rich man worked against him. Eventually he was sentenced to death. Later a governor commuted his sentence to life imprisonment and he was serving his term at the state penitentiary in Milledgeville. A lynch mob was organized by some of Marietta's finest citizens. They drove to Milledgeville and broke Leo out of jail, they took him back to Marietta, which had been Mary Phagan's hometown, and hanged the poor man.

Aunt Sara had found out one very interesting thing. Just before he was lynched, Leo Frank gave his wedding ring to one of his killers and asked that it be given to his wife. Incredibly, one of the lynch mob respected his wish and his wife Lucille got the ring. Every time Sara told the story she had a tear in her eye.

When many years later, practically on his deathbed, the man who had been a janitor at the factory confessed to the crime, Sam clipped the story out of *The Atlanta Constitution* and mailed it to Sara who was by then living in Washington, D.C. By that time Sara's daughter Jan, who had stayed in Virginia, had a good government job in Washington, and she was able to set Sara up in an apartment near her own. Sam had come to miss her after she had moved away. After Aunt Mary, of course, Sara was Sam's favorite aunt.

And what about the other Rosenbloom sister, his mother Annie? While Abe was alive, she kept moving them from one apartment to another, always trying to shave some dollars off the monthly rent. They would stay at a place for a few months, but then she'd get another wild idea that things would be better a few blocks away.

Sam felt sorry for his father, always sweet and gentle and putting up with Annie's crazy notions. Sam always believed that her forcing him to borrow a truck and move so many times the heavy furniture she was determined to keep led to the heart attack that killed Abe in his early fifties.

Of course, to be honest, Abe's habit of smoking two or three packs of strong Turkish cigarettes every day and drinking almost a dozen Coca-Colas daily had to contribute to the failure of his good heart.

After Abe died, Annie kept on moving. Sam recalled that she had even moved to Marie's house one time, but the day came when Marie came home from her job at Rich's and couldn't find Annie. A week or so later Marie discovered that Annie had rented a room from a family five or six houses down on Marie's block.

No matter where she was living Annie kept stirring up trouble with her sisters. Saying untrue things about one sister to another was her way of causing and keeping alive constant feuds among them. Sam couldn't recall a single time when all of the sisters were speaking to one another.

Sam thought, "What a shame. What a waste." They could have all cared for and loved each other. How sad to live alone and not have anyone to care about you or even to care for you. Even though he himself lived alone, he was certain that he had people who cared, especially his family, small as it was.

"Family is everything," Sam said to himself. It brought to mind Thanksgiving. That was one day of the year when what was left of his family gathered together at his nephew's house. His nephew, Marie's son, his wife, their children and grandchildren, Sam and his daughter and her husband, his sister Marie— all of them came together as a family to celebrate. It was a yearly ritual.

It saddened him to think he was the last of the Robkins. No sons alive to carry on the name. Still, his daughter said that as long as he was alive, she'd see to it that he got to Thanksgiving with the rest. Even in a wheelchair or, God forbid, on a stretcher, she would get him there.

Chapter Nine

Sam heard the sound of a diesel engine and the hiss of air brakes. He looked up and saw that a bus had stopped and some people were getting off. A bus had been pulling out earlier when he had crossed Virginia and taken a seat on the bench. The coming of this second bus told Sam that he had been resting there for fifteen or twenty minutes. "Time to move, Sam," he murmured.

He went to get up. He managed to rise a little, but then fell back on the bench's hard seat. He rested a second, took a deep breath, and then gave a big push, using his cane, and stood. When he felt steady and balanced, he began to walk slowly down Highland away from Virginia.

The first building he passed was a bar called Moe's & Joe's. It had been there for as long as Sam could remember. Next to it was a small space housing a real estate office. Then came George's Tavern, a place gussied up with a fake hedge outside and a couple of wrought iron tables, each with checkered red and white tablecloths. No matter how they tried to fancy things up, it was still just George's Tavern, a real neighborhood bar. The television show called *Archie's Place* (a spinoff of *All in the Family*) always made Sam think of George's.

Not that Sam had ever been in either Moe's & Joe's or George's Tavern. Neither he nor Hannah were drinkers. He thought of the old saying: "Jews don't drink. They eat!"

He was walking slowly now because his legs were beginning to feel heavy and small twinges of pain were coming from his knees. He was beside the show window of what had been until recently Jimmy Watson's Barber Shop. It had been the last of the original businesses to close. Sam remembered that his daughter had told him a few months before she'd seen a *Going Out of Business* sign in Jimmy's window. Sam guessed that since the neighborhood had become what his daughter called "trendy" the rent must have become too high for Jimmy. More change.

Jimmy's place was now some sort of store selling high-end women's clothes. He could see mannequins with bright-colored dresses and high heels. "Pretty wild stuff, if you ask me," Sam thought, but of course he smiled as it crossed his mind that no one was asking him.

He leaned close to the shop window and saw price tags on the mannequins that shocked him. Everything nowadays was, to his way of thinking, too expensive and completely out of whack.

His daughter did all his shopping now. Whenever he asked her about the prices she paid, he could not believe what things cost now. She laughed and said he was still judging by what he had paid back in the sixties. And he would always tell her that he remembered when a loaf of bread cost ten cents, day-old a nickel.

Seeing Jimmy Watson's barber shop turned into a store for overpriced clothes and shoes took Sam's mind back to those days nearly fifty years before when he brought his sons to Jimmy's for their first haircuts and how through the years Alan and Cary had ridden their bikes there to get their hair cut. He smiled remembering how they both had resisted when many of their friends went through the hippie phase. At the beginning of every summer they had Jimmy turn their already short hair into crew cuts.

They were both popular kids and made a lot of good friends in their years at Grady High. He felt a second of sadness thinking how evident and widespread were the friendships his sons had when he recalled the crowds of young men and women who came to their funerals. Young men and women, Sam thought. Young. Forty-year-olds. To Sam that was still young.

He stood by the doorway of what had been Jimmy Watson's and looked north farther along Highland Avenue. He could see the hardware store, and beyond it a red hook and ladder truck in the driveway of the firehouse. He knew if he kept walking all the way to Amsterdam Avenue he would see other buildings he could remember—the old post office on the other side of the street and near it the building where Vrono's Supermarket had been. He knew he could not even think of walking that far. It was time to turn back and head for home. His tired legs, growing heavier, were telling him so.

But standing there he could see the new sign and modernized storefront of what had been one of his favorite places on the street, Highland Hardware. He wondered if they had updated the inside of the store the way they had the outside. The old place had dark hardwood floors that squeaked when you walked on them, and a pungent smell that hit you as soon as you crossed the threshold. He could almost sense it still—an odor that was a mixture of years of dust and grease and floor wax. It was not a bit foul. In fact, it had always been pleasing to him.

Sam could not count how many times he had come to the place for light bulbs or a box of carpet tacks or some other small item. Now there were giant chains like Home Depot or Lowe's with stores the size of football fields, selling everything from lumber and nails all the way up to household appliances. Back when he was steadier on his feet, he had gone to one of those stores with his son-in-law. Just walking around, the size of the place had made him dizzy.

Sam was feeling warm. Like most April days in Atlanta, this one was giving off signs of the summer to come. Always health-conscious, Sam was one of the millions of Americans who had become serious water drinkers, people who had added words like *hydration* and *hydrated* to their vocabulary.

Between the day's growing heat and the exercise he had already had, not to mention the way some of his medications left his mouth bone dry, Sam knew he needed to drink some water. In his rush to get of the house, he had forgotten to slip a plastic bottle of water in his pocket.

He looked across Highland and saw a shop near Virginia he was sure would have a refrigerated case with bottles of water in it. Because of both the traffic going past in a heavy stream and how slowly he moved, Sam did not give even a single thought of jaywalking.

Slowly he turned and started back to the intersection of Highland and Virginia where there was a traffic light that would give him time to get across.

Chapter Ten

Waiting for the light to change, Sam thought about how good would be the drink of water he was going to have. He had always known that water was good for you, but when his doctor told him how crucial drinking plenty of water every day was to his kidneys and a lot of other benefits he would get, Sam was totally convinced.

Of course, having to go to the bathroom ten or twelve times a day was bothersome, but he had vowed he would do whatever it took to stay as healthy as possible. One thing that worried him was that someday he might have to wear what he called a diaper and what the TV commercials called adult undergarments. It had happened to Hannah in the nursing home when towards the end she lost control of her bladder.

The light finally changed, and the attempt to get to the other side of Highland Avenue as quickly as possible took a lot out of him. He could feel himself getting low on energy. He really needed the water. He stood still for a moment to rest and recover from the effort of crossing the street.

A few slow steps to his right brought him to the door of a store he had known years before when it was a little grocery. He was pleased that he could recall the name of the couple who ran to store years before: Klein. Back then it had been Klein's Fine Produce. He smiled as he remembered how people used to say they were going to shop at Klein's Fine. Now the place was—what else?—a coffee shop.

A little bell tinkled as he stepped inside. That had not changed. He'd bet the bell had been part of the place forever.

He looked up at the sign over the counter at the rear of the shop. It had letters big enough that he did not need his reading glasses. Good thing. In his hurry to get out of the house and start his walk, he had forgotten to bring them, too.

The sign was still not easy to read, but he was pretty sure that the name of the place was Coffee Beanz. With a *Z*. Like all the other stores and shops in the area it had to have a clever name. At least it wasn't one of the big chains. Once when he was out with his daughter, they had stopped at a Starbucks. He could not believe the prices there. He told his daughter he'd just as soon drink instant Nescafé at home—at least there the cost of the coffee was reasonable.

Right away he felt good about the place. The air conditioning was on and the shop was pleasantly cool. Another thing that pleased him was the wonderful aroma of coffee being brewed. He looked around and spotted the reason why he had come there. Just inside the door was a narrow refrigerated case that held Cokes and other soft drinks and clear bottles of water.

He opened the case's sliding door and took out a bottle of spring water. Then he noticed the price label on the shelf: a dollar and seventy-nine cents. Sam almost put it back, surprised at the cost. It was just water, for God's sake. It didn't have the secret formula and a cup of sugar like the Cokes near it. At home his daughter kept his refrigerator stocked with six-packs of water. He wondered how much she paid for them. He hoped the bottles back at St. Charles were not as expensive as the one in his hand.

Still, Sam knew that he really needed that water. He would pay whatever it took. He reached back and patted his left rear pocket. At least he had not forgotten his wallet.

The only other person in the shop was a pretty young woman behind the counter. "Welcome to Beanz," she said.

Sam nodded, acknowledging her greeting. He stepped to a table, noticing how low the chairs around it were. He knew that if he sat down he would have trouble getting up. He also knew he had to sit a while and rest again. "What the hell," he thought. " I'll worry about it later." He set his bottle of water on the table, hooked his cane on the back of a chair, took off his cap, and, holding on to the edge of the table, slowly eased himself down. It was a sudden relief to be off his feet.

The young woman watched and seemed to know how much effort the simple act of sitting down cost Sam.

Sam unscrewed the cap of his bottle of water and took the drink he so badly needed. He drank nearly half the bottle before he set it down. The woman— to him just a girl—asked in a friendly voice if he lived in the neighborhood.

He knew why she asked. An old man was an oddity. The Highlands was a place where you very seldom saw elderly people. It had become an area where many young professional types had moved in. You saw a lot of young married couples with kids in strollers, many of them with small dogs on leashes.

Sam answered her question by saying he had been living down on St. Charles Place for more than fifty years. He saw a surprised look on her face. She said, "I don't think I know anyone who's lived in the same place for fifty years."

Sam did not usually get into conversations like this. Under normal circumstances he would have come in, bought his water, and been on his way. Not today. He was tired and needed some rest to gather his strength for the remainder of his walk. The girl seemed eager to speak with him. Probably, Sam thought, she had never had a customer so old.

Sam sipped a little bit of water and said, "It's almost lunch time. You must have a lot to do. Don't worry about me."

She laughed, "A lot to do? It's Wednesday. I'm only busy on the weekend. Sometimes on Saturday or Sunday, you wouldn't believe how crowded this place can get. When it's slow like this I'm glad to get the chance to sit and visit with my customers. It's a break in the routine."

While she was saying this she had come around from behind the counter and sat down opposite him at the small table. Up close, Sam could see how good-looking she was. The long black apron she wore emphasized the curviness of her slender figure. She reminded him of his daughter's friend Arlene.

"My name's Kimberly. What's yours?"

"Sam Robkin. I know you've been brought up to be polite to your elders and you'll want to call me Mr. Robkin. Don't. Just call me Sam."

"Okay, Sam. Sam it is." Then her dark eyes flashed as a thought seemed to strike her. "You said you've lived around here for fifty years. Maybe you knew my grandparents when this place was their grocery store, Eva and Louis Klein."

"Klein's Fine Produce. Sure, I knew them," Sam answered. "I traded here a lot."

That brought a big smile to Kimberly's face. Her smile broadened when Sam said he had known Eva as a young girl when she lived down on the south side. What he did not say was that as a young kid he had had a tremendous crush on Eva from the first day he met her. Her family had moved in around the corner from where the Robkins were living in a house on Powell Street just off Boulevard.

Sam had never seen a naturally blonde Jewish girl before and thought Eva was beautiful. Along with her good looks, she had a sweet nature and a confident way about her. Sam at the time was a shy kid and Eva never knew how taken with her he was.

Looking back, he knew what he lacked then was self-esteem, something he guessed from hearing constant talk on television about the need for that quality. He was sure that his mother Annie was the source of that lack.

Kimberly was genuinely delighted to learn that Sam had known her grandmother as a young girl.

She had never heard very many stories from her grandparents about their early days.

Just then the little bell gave its tinny jingle. A young couple came in. Kimberly jumped up, saying, "Excuse me, Sam. Business. Don't go away." She went behind the counter, greeted the new customers, and took their orders for some coffees to go. The names of the kinds of coffee they wanted sounded strange to Sam.

As Kimberly drew the couple's drinks from a hissing machine, Sam finished his water and saw a sign pointing to the restrooms toward the back of the shop.

Sam was surprised at how good he felt and how easily he rose from the table. He took his cane and slowly made his way to the restroom. Funny how good talking to a pretty woman made a man feel. Good for the spirit and body both.

Chapter Eleven

By the time Sam returned, Kimberly's customers had left the store and she was waiting for him at his table. He saw that she had brought another bottle of water and set it at his place across from her. With a little struggle he got seated again and they resumed their conversation.

Kimberly was very interested in hearing from Sam stories about how life had been years ago when her grandparents had their grocery store. She was eager to learn what he could tell her about the Jewish community in south Atlanta where Eva's family and Sam's had lived and how that whole community seemed to have moved almost completely north to the nearby areas of Morningside, Lenox Road, and Johnson Estates.

Sam told her how Jewish life in the early twentieth century had been centered around Boulevard and Memorial Drive, but when the interstate was built through downtown and the Atlanta Stadium for the Braves was developed, most of the old area was cleared. That was when it seemed that the whole community moved north.

He laughed when he told her that his sons used to tell people that their father had been born on third base. That was where the old Piedmont Hospital had been before it, too, moved.

Sam's mentioning of his sons led Kimberly to ask how many children he had. He had to tell her that both sons were dead and the only child he had left was his daughter. When Sam spoke about the deaths of his sons, Kimberly lowered her eyes and said softly, "I'm sorry for your losses. It must be terrible for a parent to go through that."

Sam was moved by her expression of sadness. He nodded and said, "Yes, terrible indeed. May nothing like that ever happen to you."

Gracefully she steered the conversation back to the old days in south Atlanta. Sam told her that his grandfather, Avram Rosenbloom, was a very devout man who kept kosher and was one of the founders of the synagogue Ahavath Achim. Of course, that was long before the congregation had moved to the north side of the city.

Kimberly said, "The AA." Everyone always used the initials when they spoke of the synagogue.

"That's where I went to Hebrew school and was confirmed."

She looked up as the bell at the front door sounded again. She excused herself and went to the counter where she made sandwiches for the two young men who had entered, making bright conversation with them as she made and served them their lunch at a table next to where Sam was sitting.

As he waited for Kimberly to come back, Sam found that all the talk about the synagogue reminded him how religion was not all that important to him personally. He knew that plenty of men as they got older started to be active, making minyan, showing up for Sabbath, even davening, but not Sam. He and Hannah had always attended services on the High Holidays, but that was it.

Two things had soured him. First of all, the old man who prepared Sam for his bar mitzvah's *haftorah* was a mean old codger from the old country who barely spoke English. It was hard to understand him. If Sam made a mistake in reading the Hebrew, the cruel bastard—that's how Sam thought of the man—would crack him across the knuckles with a stick he used as a cane. Sam never forgot how much those blows hurt. If being religious meant acting like him, no thanks.

The other incident happened when Sam was very young. One of his grandfathers, Abe's father, had

died. The custom then was for members of the synagogue to wash the body and wrap it in a shroud.
Then the body was kept overnight and the mourners
came to sit shiva. Sam's sleep was troubled that night,
thinking about the shroud-wrapped form in the front
room.

The next day, when the others had gone with the
body to the cemetery, one of the older men had
grabbed Sam, and made him take the board the body
had lain on out to the yard and wash it. Scrubbing that
board while his mind filled with thoughts of the corpse
gave Sam nightmares for years after. He associated it
with other Jewish customs he came to hate, especially
how at the end of funerals each mourner took the
shovel from a pile of graveside dirt and pitched earth
and small rattling stones down on the coffin.

Still, he and Hannah thought of themselves as good
Jews. They made sure that each of their sons had bar
mitzvahs and that their daughter, like Kimberly, went
to Hebrew school and was confirmed at the AA.

By the time Kimberly returned, Sam had shaken
off his bad memories and tried to lighten things up
by asking the young woman questions about herself.

She told him she was single, but, with almost a
giggle, still looking. Sam said he wished he knew a
nice Jewish boy for her. Kimberly laughed as she said,
"You sound like my mother."

Sam found himself wondering how could such a beautiful, sweet girl not have been grabbed already. Things were really different nowadays. Young people these days seemed to have so many issues. They were getting married much later than when he and Hannah were young. The average age for getting married back then must have been eighteen or nineteen. And back then they were encouraged by everyone in their families to get started right away having children.

Kimberly told Sam she had always wanted to own her own business just like Eva and Louis. Her grandparents had sold the store and retired to Florida when Kimberly was a little girl, but they had held on to the deed to the property. Over the years a lot of businesses had rented the space there on Highland Avenue.

When Kimberly graduated from the University of Georgia, her parents, who had inherited the store, handed her the keys, and said, "Okay, go start a business."

Her father had done very well as an insurance broker and was able to give her seed money to start, and he had kept investing all along. Now, she told Sam, after three years she was showing a good enough profit to begin paying her father back. She told him how lucky she felt to have bought a little house further down Virginia Avenue not far from

Grady High. It had fallen into disrepair. That's why she had been able to get it at a good price. She had fixed it up. "You wouldn't believe what I've been offered for it." Sam smiled, recalling the real estate people calling him and thought, but didn't say, "I can believe it."

Chapter Twelve

Kimberly's telling him in a happy tone of voice about her little house and how, when the weather was good, she could ride her bicycle to her coffee shop, suddenly made a terrible thought come to Sam. Here was this beautiful young girl running a small business, alone in her shop—how safe could she be? It made him remember how his son, a six foot tall, 200-pound man in good shape, was not able to protect himself from an intruder who murdered him.

Kimberly saw a troubled look cross Sam's face and she asked if he was okay. Sam said he was, but a sense of concern for her safety had come to him. She gave a little laugh and said, "Now you're sounding like my father. He always things of creepy things that could happen."

Then she assured him that she was as safe as she could be in her shop. Her father had installed a security system that could bring help in minutes. There was an association of merchants who looked out for one another. The police patrolled the area very frequently. Every night she had a security guard her father employed present when she closed the shop.

"All well and good," Sam thought, but recalling what had happened to his son Cary did not leave his mind. Some more customers came in and took Kimberly away, leaving him still thinking of Cary.

Cary was murdered on the seventh of July, in 1988. The date was burned into his memory. His daughter had been the last person to speak with him. He had called her around nine o'clock to say he was still at his clothing store and he was going to stay a while to repair the front door that was sticking. His daughter had said that that didn't sound safe, but Cary had laughed and said, "Who's going to hurt me?"

It was after twelve, at the height of lunch time, and Kimberly was busy serving customers coming in for sandwiches and such. Sam sat at his small table and kept thinking about his second son.

At the time of his death, Cary was married with two small daughters, but he had been a bachelor for a long time. He had gone north at the age of twenty to work for an uncle of Hannah's who had a successful men's clothing store in New Jersey just across from Manhattan.

Cary worked hard and really took to the business. He learned a great deal about retail, and through friendship with a rep who called on the uncle's store he managed to land a job in merchandising with a very large, well-known men's clothing manufacturer in New York city. He worked even harder and moved up the ladder. His income increased. He changed jobs as opportunities came, and he wound up as a vice president at a children's clothing company.

He was doing very well and the bachelor life in Manhattan suited him. He had many relationships with women, but he always stayed single. But one day, as Sam's daughter put it, he got nabbed. Finally a woman at his workplace with whom he'd been having an affair caught him, using the oldest trick in the book: she came up pregnant.

Cary was angry and didn't agree to marry her right away. He wanted to be sure the child was his. After the paternity tests proved positive, he married the woman and the baby was born.

Three years after the first child was born, Cary's wife became pregnant again. A second beautiful daughter was born. Cary decided New York was a hard city to live in and raise children. He wanted his daughters to have a childhood like the one he had had in Atlanta.

He had acquired so much knowledge of retail and merchandising and had so many buying connections in New York that he knew he could make a go of a clothing business in Atlanta. His plan was to start off with a single store and then open a chain of boutiques that sold men's and women's clothes.

He came to Atlanta for a month and stayed at his sister's house. Together they researched the demographics of areas in Atlanta and its suburbs.

He moved his family south and took an apartment in a community near where Sam's daughter lived. Cary and his wife were thrilled at how spacious their apartment was compared to the one they lived in up in New York.

He opened what he planned to be his first store in an older suburb. He worked hard and, as he had been sure it would be, the store was successful from its first days. It was beginning to pay off when the disaster of his murder ended his dreams.

Early that July morning the county police phoned his daughter and told her to come to the store. All they had said was that an accident had happened. When Sam's daughter and son-in-law got there, they learned that Gary had been shot in what seemed like a robbery.

Sam's memories of the days that followed were sketchy. Alan was still alive, and he and Sam's daughter had the terrible task of arranging Cary's funeral. All he remembered was how overcome Hannah and he were. Her grief was profound, as was his, and they went through the days after Cary's murder in a daze. He wondered at how they made it through it all. Thank God for Alan and his daughter. Without them he and Hannah could not have survived.

Of course, Cary's wife, who had never wanted to come to Atlanta in the first place, soon after the funeral moved with her daughters back to New York. Sam's daughter traveled frequently up to New York often as the girls were growing up. She wanted them to know that they still had family and would never be forgotten. Over the years she became more than their aunt. She was like a big sister. She still talked with them over the phone every week, chatting and laughing together, talking about clothes and shoes and, of course, boys.

While Sam was remembering Cary's story, Kimberly had been bustling about the store, taking care of the needs of her customers through what was the busy period of lunchtime. Every now and again she came over to see if Sam was all right.

Chapter Thirteen

At last the rush of customers ended and Kimberly came and sat down at Sam's table. He made a point of shaking off his sad memories of Cary's death and resolved to be as bright and cheerful as he could for Eva's granddaughter. She was being extremely kind.

When the bell at the front door stopped ringing, he found himself back in conversation with the bright young girl, eager to learn more of the old days in Atlanta.

Sam remarked on how busy the shop had been for the past half hour or so. He told Kimberly that seeing her rushing about serving food and drinks to her customers reminded him of his father and mother's store on Powell Street.

With a laugh he told her his children always said that their grandfather Abe had invented the notion of a fast-food takeout restaurant with a drive-up window.

"Really?" Kimberly said. "Tell me about it."

Sam told her how the store was across the street from the Fulton Bag and Cotton Mill. Kimberly said she knew the place. It had been closed years before and had recently been developed as an apartment and condominium complex. One of her college friends had just moved there.

Sam told Kimberly that back in the days before World War I the mill was one of the biggest employers in the city. The mill ran three shifts. Some of the workers would rush out at lunchtime and cross over to Abe and Annie's store.

Abe had been very friendly with one of the guards who worked at the mill. One day the man showed Abe some loose bricks in the wall. You could pull them out, set them on the sidewalk, and look in and see the looms. The noise was deafening.

Abe thought about those loose bricks and one day he and Annie made about forty sandwiches, wrapped them in waxed paper, and carried them across Powell Street to the wall of the mill. Abe made a separate trip, carrying over a big tub of ice filled with bottles of Coca-Cola. Word spread among the workers and they came to the opening. That first day Abe sold out the food and drinks in twenty minutes.

It became a regular noontime thing. Management let this happen, pleased that the workers were not leaving the premises and coming back late. They even set aside a room near the opening that had tables and chair where the workers could eat their lunch.

When he wasn't in school, Sam would help out by pulling a wagon on which the tub of sodas was set across Powell Street to the wall of the mill. It was a profitable venture for months, but it ended when Annie got into a fight with one of the managers who had a bricklayer come in and seal the hole in the mill wall. One more time, Sam thought of how Annie's actions always managed to foul things up.

Sam was conscious of time passing, knowing he still had a long way to go before he reached his house. He got out his wallet and offered to pay for the water he had drunk, saying he had to be on his way.

Kimberly said, "Oh, no. It's on the house, Sam. I know how important it is for you to finish your walk. I know if I call a taxi, you'd refuse. Let me make you a latte and give you something to eat. It'll give you some energy. If Eva was here, she wouldn't let you leave without a little nosh."

Sam normally would have refused, but she was right. Eva would certainly have put something to eat in front of him. To be served food during a visit was a Jewish custom Sam had been raised to always say yes to.

A few minutes later, Kimberly had put on the table a small plate with a blueberry muffin and set down a cup that was mostly hot milk with just a trace of coffee. He had to admit that the food and drink hit the spot, even if he was just being polite.

Kimberly sat down across from him and said, "One more story, Sam, and then you can go."

Sam remembered that Kimberly had said she knew Fulton Bag and Cotton Mill, because one of her friends had bought a condominium there after the place had been converted. He asked her if she knew the Atlanta landmark nearby, Oakland Cemetery. When Kimberly said she'd never been there, Sam told her she should visit Oakland some nice afternoon. Some of her ancestors were surely buried there. There was a big Jewish section crowded with tombstones, some of them very elaborate and beautiful. He told her how his daughter had gone there a couple of times and found the gravesites of Rosenblooms and Robkins, even some Robkinskys who lived before the family shortened up the name as many immigrants did as part of becoming Americans.

Sam had brought up the topic of the cemetery because as a boy he and his sister and all the neighborhood kids went over to the cemetery and used it as a playground. It was walled in and had many paved roads, some of them like a city street with the mausoleums of the rich lined up.

It was the only wide open space in Cabbagetown where they could run around and play games. Back then there was still a lot of property not yet used for burials. On nice spring days some kids even flew kites there.

What Sam wanted Kimberly to know was an incident that was clear in his memory, how from time to time a red-haired girl older than him and his friends would come riding through the grounds on a small horse, followed by a man on a bigger horse. The man was dressed in an old Confederate army uniform. The kids all guessed the man came as a sort of guard for the girl. They must have come from a nearby neighborhood nicer than Cabbage-town.

Sam and his friends would run after the girl and try to talk with her, but she would just keep on riding and totally ignoring them. He remembered that the guard had called her Peggy.

Kimberly said she could see clearly in her imagination the girl, holding her head high and having nothing to do with a bunch of younger boys. It was something she might have done herself.

Sam laughed and said, "What Peggy didn't know was that we weren't interested in her at all. What we cared about was the horse. I remember she called the horse Nelly."

Sam had told his daughter about the girl and the horse. When she had visited Oakland Cemetery, she told the story to one of the guides there. He told Sam's daughter that they could verify Sam's memory.

"It turned out," Sam said, "That red-headed girl named Peggy was Margaret Mitchell."

Kimberly said, "The woman who wrote *Gone With the Wind*?"

"Yep. And what's more, when she died Margaret Mitchell was buried at Oakland. You can visit her grave there."

Telling the story to Kimberly gave Sam pleasure. In telling it he forgot for a moment how tired he was and how far he still had to go to get home, but only for a moment. He sipped the last of his latte, wiped his mouth with a crumpled napkin, and once again reached for his wallet. And once again, Kimberly refused to let him pay.

Sam put on his cap, reached for his cane and, using the table for support, stood up. He felt shaky and Kimberly reached out to steady him. She walked with him as he slowly made his way to the shop's door.

Kimberly hugged him and said, "Come back again, Sam, but don't try walking here. Get your daughter to drive you. I really look forward to meeting her. I'll make her the best mocha frappuccino she ever had. Come back again."

Bad as he felt, it pleased Sam to hear her say, "Come back." How many 88-year old men had a beautiful girl in her twenties calling after them?

Kimberly's hug had surprised and slightly embarrassed Sam. He guessed the embarrassment came out of his past. He wasn't—what was the phrase he heard on TV all the time? Oh, yes, "touchy-feely." That, too, probably was because of Annie and her lack of affection.

As the door closed behind him, Sam heard the little bell give its ring. He hoped he would hear it again someday.

Chapter Fourteen

On the sidewalk, Sam was out in the sun again. He squinted and pulled down the short visor on his cap to shield his eyes. It did not help much. He walked slowly toward the corner of Virginia and Highland. There was a shady spot in front of some stores around the corner on Virginia. He turned, stood to rest a while, and glanced in the show window of a store there. He couldn't remember what the store had once sold, but now it seemed to be some sort of an antique shop. In the window he could see old furniture and lamps.

Something on a shelf caught his eye. He leaned forward to get a better look. He was taken aback. There it was—a bronze Art Deco statuette of a nude woman. He saw it was exactly like the one he had given his sister some fifty or more years ago for a wedding present. He had bought it at Brentano's in New York where he had worked.

Brentano's was a famous bookstore, but it also had other businesses. Brentano's had an engraving department that did stationery and invitations for the wealthy people of Park and Fifth Avenues. Sam was a delivery boy, taking neatly wrapped packages of stationery to the big mansions and tall brownstones in the city.

Brentano's also sold *objets d'art*. When he first saw the statue at the store, he knew it would delight Marie. It was pretty expensive, but Sam loved Marie and saved until he could buy it just before she got married.

Standing before the shop's window, looking past his reflection at the statue on the shelf, he remembered that his daughter had spoken about Marie's statue not very long ago. It struck Sam then that this statue he was looking at might just be the very one he had bought back in the late twenties.

It seemed that when Marie was going to move from her house on Morningside to an apartment after her husband died, she had called members of the family and asked if they wanted to see what she had to give away.

When his daughter went to Marie's, she saw the statue and raved about it, saying she had just the spot for it in her own house. His daughter's house was a very artful mix of old and new. She had many antique pieces mixed throughout. Marie was happy to give it to her, reminding his daughter that it had been a gift from her father and to be sure to take good care of it.

As Sam's daughter told it to him, a few months later Marie had phoned his daughter. Marie was very embarrassed, close to tears, and with difficulty got around to saying she would have to ask his daughter to give the statue back.

His daughter had sensed how troubled Marie was and made it easy for her, saying, " Yes, of course. I'll bring it back in the morning."

It seemed that Marie's son, Sam's nephew, had demanded that she call Sam's daughter and get the statue back. He must have thought about it a long time and figured that the statue bought so long ago would have increased in value and would be worth a lot.

A while later, his daughter learned quite by accident that when *The Antiques Road Show* had come to Atlanta, his nephew's wife and her daughter had taken it there to be appraised. They were told that hundreds of statues like the one they had brought were made back in the twenties and it wasn't worth very much at all. Sam thought maybe they had come here to Virginia and Highland and sold it for what little they could get.

Sam had been disturbed when his daughter told him about the statue, but his daughter was not troubled a bit. She just said some people's greed sometimes exceeds their manners. And that was that.

Shaking his head slightly, Sam stepped away from the shop window. He knew he would have to get moving again. He still had a long way to go. Even with the long periods of rest that sitting at the bus stop bench and his time in the coffee shop had given him, he was not feeling good.

He crossed at the light and started down the sidewalk on the opposite side of Highland. He noticed how differently he was walking now. He had started out from St. Charles Place at a good pace, but now he was almost shuffling.

The sidewalk on this side of Highland seemed especially rough and uneven, and he feared that he might stumble and fall. "Oh boy," he thought, "that would be the end for me."

Just then two young boys came whizzing by him on skateboards, yelling, "Move it, Pops!" Startled, Sam almost lost his balance and started falling toward a lawn. He pushed his cane ahead of him and stopped the fall. The effort of staying erect cost him a good deal of his already low store of energy.

To the boys, wearing helmets and pads, he was just another obstacle. Sam forgave them. They were just being boys. They could not imagine what a fall would have done to Sam, but he could—perhaps a broken hip, a ride in an ambulance, a confrontation with his daughter, frantic at being summoned to the emergency room at Grady or some other hospital.

Despite his need to keep moving, Sam stood for a few minutes and felt his heart racing. He leaned heavily on his cane and breathed deeply, trying to get calm. He felt clammy, a cold sweat covering him. Slowly he started walking again, this time thinking about every step he managed to take. He knew he would have to find a place to stop and rest again.

Even feeling as bad as he did, Sam took notice of the businesses on this side of Highland Avenue. He passed what had been a gas station where he had often filled up his car in the past. Now it was something called a wine bar.

Sam came to the corner of Greenwood and Highland. He had to cross over, but the curb was higher than most. He knew he could not manage the long step down. He turned and went down Greenwood a little ways till he came to a driveway that was level with the street. He crossed over and turned back to Highland.

He came to the building at the corner and remembered that it had been another drugstore, bigger and fancier than Dr. Shackleford's. Now it was a Vietnamese restaurant, something he never thought he would see on Highland Avenue. Passing it, he saw a sign that said it had been voted "Best Vietnamese Restaurant" in the city in *Atlanta Magazine*. He wondered how many Vietnamese restaurants there could be for this one to be voted best. Sam knew that Atlanta had become a truly international city with many neighborhoods of different ethnic groups. When he was young the only immigrants he remembered were from Europe, mainly from Russia like his grandfather.

When Sam was growing up on the south side, there was one Chinese family. The parents did laundry and some form of dry cleaning and the children all stuck together, not playing with the other children. Sam thought how it must have been very lonely and difficult for them.

Sam was really struggling now. With every slow step he felt shocks of pain in his knees—"bone on bone" the doctor had said. The words echoed in Sam's mind as he felt them being translated in the reality of his body.

Looking ahead he saw an old iron park bench under an awning in front of a shop. It was probably only twenty yards away, but to Sam it seemed like miles. He made it a target. He would make it home by setting one small goal after another.

Step by step he drew closer to the bench until at last he stood in front of it. He turned and sat down with great force, almost hurling his body onto the bench. Sam felt a rush of relief, having the pressure off his aching legs. He sat for a long moment and then craned his head around to see what sort of a shop he was sitting in front of. He saw lettered on the window the place's name. It said *Peach Melba*. What could that mean?

Looking in the window, he saw women and men sitting in chairs, all covered with short cape-like cloths, getting things done to their heads. There were women at tables getting manicures. A beauty salon, Sam thought. He marveled at how the customers were a mix of men and women. Things were different when Sam was younger—women didn't go into barber shops and men didn't go into beauty salons.

Sam sensed the presence of someone standing before him. At first Sam was not sure if the person was a man or a woman. He guessed rightly that it was man, probably the thinnest man Sam had ever seen. He had blond hair, neither short nor long, but fixed in waves like a woman's. Besides tiny diamond earrings, the man definitely had cosmetics on his eyes and lips.

The man said, "Hi, my name is Jamie. I saw you when you got to the bench. Do you need any help? Can I get you anything?"

Sam was stirred as he sensed the man's kindness. He told Jamie he had gone for a walk and was struggling to get back home. He just needed to sit and rest for a while.

Jamie said, "How about some water?" Sam said yes, realizing how dry he felt.

"Back in a sec," Jamie said. He ducked into the shop and was back almost instantly with a bottle of ice-cold water. He handed it to Sam and noticed how hard it seemed for Sam to get the cap off.

"Let me help you," Jamie said, taking the bottle. "Sometimes they're really hard to unscrew." Sam took the bottle, thanked Jamie, and took a long swallow.

Jamie suggested that he come into the shop and sit inside. Even though he kept the door open, the air conditioner was running and it was nice and cool inside.

Sam thanked him and said he would come inside, but needed to wait a few minutes to gather his strength.

Jamie asked Sam how old he was and Sam told him. Jamie said, " Eighty-eight! Oh my goodness, you're incredible! My grandmother's seventy-seven and she has trouble walking from room to room! She could never walk even *one* of these blocks!"

Sam was used to people making a fuss over his age, seemingly surprised that he was still alive and walking around. Sometimes it seemed he was treated like a freak. Hearing Jamie's praise, Sam said that he now felt good enough to take Jamie's offer to go inside.

Jamie reached down to help Sam get up, but stepped back as Sam said, "Let me see if I can do it myself." Sam handed his bottle of water to Jamie, used the iron arm of the bench and his cane, and got on his feet. He felt his knees take the strain, but stepped slowly into the shop, feeling a cool breeze as he did so.

Looking to his right he saw some chairs and sofas upholstered in some wild bright-green colors. They looked soft and low. Sam knew immediately that he couldn't sit on any of them. He would be so close to the floor that he would never be able to get up again.

He saw a fairly tall chair with a narrow back near a small counter where the cash register was. It had two thin arms he knew he could use to raise himself when it was time to get up. Jamie nodded yes when Sam asked if he could sit there.

Sam was sitting up high at the front of the shop and, tired as he was, enjoyed taking the whole scene in. There was loud music playing, some girl singing words Sam couldn't make out. He smiled. "Even if I could understand the words," he thought, "I wouldn't get it."

All the people in the shop, both the customers and the employees, seemed to ignore the loud music, easily talking to each other over the sound. There was a lot of laugher, a lot of teasing of one another. It seemed a bright, happy place.

Jamie said, "I have to leave you here for a while. I have a foil coloring to do."

Sam said, "Okay," and wondered what the heck a foil coloring meant. The whole experience was a new world to Sam, being in a hair salon filled with men and women. He had driven Hannah many times for her appointments when she was no longer able to drive herself, but he'd never gone inside with her. He either drove off to run some errands or stayed outside and read the newspaper in his parked car.

Sam thought how he would like to talk with his daughter about Jamie and being in *Peach Melba* and what he was seeing there, but knew he had better not bring the subject up. His daughter would be upset about his being so worn out that he needed to rest in a beauty shop.

After a fair amount of time, maybe fifteen minutes, Jamie came back to see how Sam was doing. Even though Sam was still tired, he told Jamie was okay. Jamie didn't really believe him, hearing a tremor in Sam's voice and noticing how pale he was. Jamie asked if Sam lived far. Sam said, "Not really. Just a block or so to St. Charles Place and then about half-way down."

Jamie thought a minute and then said, "That's still pretty far. I'm with my last client and I can drive you home when I'm finished." He pointed outside the shop and there was a little two-seater bright yellow car with its top down. Sam knew that if he ever got in it his knees would never let him get out again.

He thanked Jamie and said he could make it on his own. He was determined to finish the walk he'd started. Jamie could see that the matter was very important to Sam and didn't try to argue with him.

With an effort, Sam stood up and Jamie walked beside him to the front door. He looked across Highland Avenue and saw St. Louis Place, the street next to his own.

He turned to Jamie and said, "Thank you for your kindness. I can make it from here, but I really needed the rest you gave me."

"It was my pleasure, Sam" He reached up and touched the fringe of white hair visible under Sam's cap. "Come back and I'll give you the best haircut you ever had." Then, to Sam's surprise, Jamie gave him a hug. It reminded him of how he had left Kimberly's shop with a similar hug. "Twice in one day," he thought.

Walking very slowly, taking small deliberate steps, he headed down the sidewalk, turning once to wave at Jamie standing in the doorway of *Peach Melba,* keeping Sam in sight as if to make sure he was going to be all right.

Chapter Fifteen

Not very far from Jamie's shop Sam began to feel very bad. He had taken three long rest periods—at the bus stop, at Kimberly's, and now at Jamie's—and each time he had started his walk again he had felt worse and worse. Now he was aching all over. He felt clammy with a cold sweat under his clothes. Each knee seemed to be competing with the other in giving him pain.

With footsteps measurable in inches, he reached the corner of Highland Avenue and St. Charles Place. His eyes under his glasses were filmy with tears of pain. As he stood and waited for the traffic light to change so that he could cross over, he began to give himself a mental pep talk. "Just a little more, Sam. You can make it. Keep moving." He was talking to himself like a football coach at halftime.

He got across Highland just as the green light turned to yellow. He was shaky as he stepped up over the curb and began walking down his own familiar street. He felt his whole body trembling, giving him trouble handling his cane.

At last he saw his house. A deep feeling of relief came over him, slowing down his heart that had been racing. "Almost there, Sam," he said aloud in a low voice. "You can make it. Just a little more."

He thought of what still lay before him. There was no direct path from the sidewalk to his goal, his front door. The builder had designed it so that to get to the front door you had to walk a little distance down the driveway to where a path of flagstones were set in the lawn leading to the three steps up to a small porch.

Now confident that he was going to make it home, he felt a small surge of strength. He turned left and slowly went down to driveway to where the flagstones began. He stopped at the first flat stone and rested for a minute or more before taking the first step. Pushing off with his cane, he started on the path, feeling certain now that with a little more effort he was going to reach his goal. Reaching the steps up to the porch, he put his left hand on the railing. Making sure that the cane was firmly set on each of the steps, he made his way up and stood at last before his front door.

Taking a deep breath, Sam reached in his pocket for his key. With a sinking feeling, he realized that for the first time he could ever remember he had left the house without the key in his pocket. In all the years he had driven, his keys had made a palpable weight in his pocket, but now that he no longer drove, the only key that he carried was the one to his house. Today of all days he had left without checking to make sure it was in his pocket. His mind flashed back to this morning when DelRee had distracted him as he stood at the pewter plate where he always put the key. He groaned. Maybe his daughter was right. He was so old that he was losing his grip.

There was a wicker chair on the porch near the front door. He had to sit down. He did so with more difficulty than usual, troubled now in mind as well as body. "Now what am I going to do?"he asked himself. Breathing heavily, he tried to summon up his old calmness, his old ability to work things out.

"Think, Sam," he murmured. He consciously tried to slow his breathing, knowing he had to work on regaining some semblance of the clearness of mind that had served him so well over his many, many years. Slowly he could sense his mind settling down. It was then that there flashed into his now less-troubled mind a way out of his present problem.

He recalled, thank God, how years and years ago DelRee, fearful of her own memory, had hidden a spare key on top of the light fixture over the kitchen door on the right side of the house. He realized he could use that key to get him inside where he could safely rest.

But the thought of having to leave the porch and walk down the driveway five or so yards, climb five steps, and reach up for the spare key suddenly appeared to his mind as a journey more exhausting than the long walk he had just completed. Still, he knew he had to do it. He had no other choice.

Firmly setting his cane on the porch floor, he bore down hard on the arm of the chair to get up. He straightened his body, found his balance, and began. He went down the steps to the porch very carefully and deliberately, pausing on each one, gathering his weakened strength each time. He crossed again, slowly, the flagstone path, reaching the driveway. A part of the journey was over, but much more remained. Very much more and no easier.

He looked down the driveway to his goal, the five steps up to the little landing in front of the kitchen door. He was certain that door was locked. DelRee would never leave the house without setting the lock on the door she used. He glanced up to the light fixture where victory lay in the form of the key.

Right next to the steps up to the kitchen door he could see the opening to another set of steps, ones leading down to the basement, steps that he had almost never used in all the years he lived in the house. If from time to time he had gone to the basement with a workman, he would bring the person through the inside of the house.

Finally, walking now in a true shuffle, he came to the first of the kitchen steps. He paused there and caught his breath, leaning hard on the cane to rest.

Summoning all his energy, he grabbed hold of the wrought-iron railing and with all his strength started up the five steps, suddenly steeper than he could ever remember them.

Standing at last on the small landing, Sam looked up to his left at the light fixture. He felt sure that with some effort he could reach the top of it. Sam pressed his middle torso up against the railing and raised himself almost on tiptoe.

With his trembling right hand he reached up and felt along the metal form that covered the fixture like a small flat roof. His fingers touched the key, thin and cool. He made an attempt to pick it up, trying to get his fingernails under it. His nails were too short.

"Maybe," he thought, "if I could get it to the edge of the light...." He laid his index finger on the key's widest part and began sliding it towards him. Just as he sensed it getting closer, he tried once again to get his fingernails under it. His nerves straining, his hand gave an involuntary spasm. His fingers struck the thin rim of the key.

Almost as if it had a life of its own, the key slid quickly, its notches appearing suddenly over the fixture's edge. With a feeling of near-despair, Sam watched the key tumbling toward him, felt it touch his arm lightly as it fell, heard it hit the railing with a *clink*. Sam, horrified, saw it drop, end over end, and land in the semi-darkness of the well of the basement steps.

With a moan, Sam turned so that his back was against the kitchen door. Slowly he let his body go sliding down and down until he came to rest, sitting in a slump. His cane clattered down and lay beside him.

Sam was close to tears. He was already in a state of near-exhaustion from the strain of his long walk. This accident with the key, the key that he had placed all his hopes on, seemed to Sam to be a final blow—to come so near and then see all his hope in the form of that key go dropping down to the bottom of the basement stairs.

He sat with his head lowered for a long time, his eyes closed, his mind empty. He knew one thing only—it would be totally beyond his strength to reverse his course, to go down the kitchen stairs and then the basement ones. Never in a million years, if he got that far, could he do the impossible—climb up again to where he now sat, a crumpled, broken man.

Sam sat on the small landing for what was almost ten full minutes. His mind became overwhelmed with anxiety. His imagination had him dying there on the steps, his body not found for a full day. "What am I going to do?" he kept muttering.

Then he lifted his head as he heard some faint noises. They sounded like a door opening and closing. He looked across the way to his neighbor's backyard just in time to see the housekeeper over there come out carrying a large black trash bag. She was about to put the bag in a wheeled cart she would take to the curb when she happened to glance over and see Sam slumped against his kitchen door.

She noticed him just at the instant he tried to call out to her, but his voice was too weak. It didn't matter. She had seen him and was now hurrying across the yard and the driveway to where he was.

Sam tried to remember her name. DelRee had brought her in to meet him one time when they'd been in the kitchen having coffee together. All he could remember was that she was Mexican and spoke very little English.

The little woman ran up the steps and crouched down at Sam's side. "Mr. Sam," he heard her say, "you okay?"

In a thin voice he barely recognized as his own, he said, "No. Please help me. I dropped the door key. It fell down there." He pointed down to the basement steps.

The woman nodded and said, "Okay, I go." She ran down the kitchen door steps, spun, and raced down the basement ones, stooped over, and got the key. She raced back up and, with a flashing smile, showed Sam the key as it lay in the palm of her small hand.

Sam tried to match her smile, but his face was ashen and he seemed on the point of collapse. She saw his distress and said, "Oh, no! Mr. Sam, hold on!"

She helped him reach up with his right hand to grasp the railing. Then she crouched down, put her arms around his left side, and lifted. Sam was amazed at her strength. Almost holding his full weight, she unlocked the kitchen door and let them both in. Sam suddenly felt better. The window air conditioner in the den had cooled the whole downstairs.

She helped Sam cross the kitchen and into the den where his recliner was. She helped Sam turn, and he fell heavily into the chair. Sam felt a sense of security and relief to be home at last.

The woman said, "Can I get you something, Mr. Sam?"

In a weak voice, Sam said, "Please get me a bottle of water from the fridge."

When she came back with the water, he took her hand and said, "I want to thank you so much. You saved me. I don't know what I would've done without you."

She understood what he was saying and a big smile came over her face. "*De nada*. You need anything else, Mr. Sam?"

"No, really. Not a thing. You can go back now. I'll rest a while, and I'll be all right."

She smiled again and said, "Okay." She put the key on the small table beside his chair. "Okay. I go now." Then she left by the kitchen door.

Sam sat quietly thinking and he felt that his heart had stopped racing. He finished drinking the bottle of water and was very still but thinking hard.

He reached over for the old black phone that was there on the table where his rescuer had left the key. He dialed. When his daughter picked up the phone, he said, "Natalie, don't talk. Just listen." But of course she did talk and said, "What's wrong? You sound upset."

Sam said, "I told you not to talk. Listen to me, Natalie. I'm ready."

"Ready? Ready for what?"

"To move, to make the arrangements, to do what needs to be done. Sell this house. I'm ready to come live with you."

Acknowledgments

I want to express my deep gratitude to Ruth Windham for her substantial support, both editorial and otherwise.

Thanks to my devoted husband for his advice and assistance in copy editing.

I must thank all my friends, especially the ones I made many years ago at Grady High School, who will notice that I relocated Shackelford's Drugs. Special thanks to Dennis King, Lane Wolbe, John Stephens and Tom Dell for their efforts in keeping together the Grady community. Tom deserves a special mention for his superb colorization of the cover photograph. Thanks to my dearest friend Linda Burdine Price for being so supportive and helpful to me in this project, and for just being my friend for 57 years.

I am grateful to Phyllis Eisen for her ongoing encouragement and support as this book took shape.

She is one of the kindest and most caring people I have ever known, and she continues to inspire me.

Thanks to Laura Ellis of Studio Ellis for her patience in developing the cover design and to Butch Self for the author photograph, as well as to all the staff at BookLogix for the production of the book.

I especially want to thank my mother who was a voracious reader. I'm saddened that she's not here to read this book. I hope she would have been proud of me, but I'm certain she would have a great deal to say.

Letter to a Beloved Teacher

Dear Mr. Sanders,

You are gone but not forgotten. You are lovingly remembered by many people whom you taught for your personality, your quirkiness, and your teaching methods.

BUT, Mr. Sanders, I just want you to know that I have never needed to know the alignment of the planets since leaving high school.

I will sign off by repeating: Mr. Sanders, you were loved by all.

Fondly,
Natalie Grude

Sam, around 12 years old,
with his sister, around 11 years old.

Sam's father standing in front of his car.

Sam in the goat cart his father
had built for him and his sister.

Sam, around 8 or 9 years old,
riding in the sidecar of his father's motorcycle.

Sam looking dapper in the 1940s.

Sam walking with his
two sons in downtown Atlanta (1944).

Sam and his daughter,
around 6 months old, on Boulevard (1944).

Sam in his late 50s relaxing at home.

Sam's mother and her three sisters
(left to right): Lottie, his mother Anna, Sara, and Mary.

Sam on his 91st birthday when he lived with his daughter.